OPEN TAB

JA Armstrong

CHAPTER ONE

The warmth of the bed and the body pressed against her invited Fallon to stay right where she was. Nearly a lifetime of living in Whiskey Springs, Vermont had never helped Fallon to adapt to the freezing winter temperatures. She savored the last few moments of her cozy cocoon made of blankets and flesh. She inhaled a long breath and let it go, extricated herself from a tangle of arms and legs, and went in search of the clothes she'd shed hours ago.

"You're leaving?"

Fallon stepped into her jeans and zipped them up. "Probably a good idea," she replied evenly. She felt more than heard the woman in the bed shift to look at her.

"Now? Where do you need to be?"

"I don't need to *be* anywhere. That doesn't mean I should *be* here."

"Come back to bed, Fallon."

Fallon slipped on her bra and turned to regard the woman behind her. She'd known Andi Maguire since childhood. This arrangement was a new evolution in their relationship. Relationship? This was hardly a relationship. It was an *arrangement*. Fallon had spent her teenage years fantasizing about the woman lying in the bed. She never expected to find herself in Andi Maguire's arms. In those days, Andi was Andi Sherman, a tall, blonde goddess destined for movie stardom; that's what Fallon had imagined late at night when she would close her eyes and pretend that it was Andi's hand touching her and not her own. How many people ever got to realize their teenage fantasy? Fallon guessed few. She preferred an arrangement to a relationship.

Andi propped herself up on an elbow and let her eyes roam over Fallon's form appreciatively. "He won't be home until tomorrow."

Fallon nodded. *But he will be home.* She pulled a worn woolen sweater over her head and smiled at the older woman. *Dean would shit his pants.* Her older brother had pined over Andi Sherman throughout high school. The thought brought Fallon a degree of inappropriate satisfaction. Dean and Andi were six years older than her. She'd always felt she needed to compete with the legacy of her older brother. He seemed to accomplish every goal he set; every goal except conquering the likes of one Andi Sherman.

"What are you grinning about?" Andi asked.

"Just remembering something?"

"Oh?"

Fallon chuckled. She remembered plenty about the hours they had just shared. Parts of her body recalled it more vividly than others. She dropped down on the bed beside Andi and kissed her softly.

"Stay," Andi requested.

"I don't think that's the best idea," Fallon said.

"Why not? It's cold out there."

Andi sat up and let the blanket fall away from her. Fallon sucked in an uneasy breath. It would be easy to fall back into Andi's arms, to disappear for a few more hours in the sounds and scents that still lingered in her senses.

Tempting. Fallon kissed Andi one last time. "I need to get to work."

Andi knew that was a lie. *Murphy's Law* would hardly be busy at three o'clock on a Tuesday. The small, local pub was Fallon's pride and joy. Andi sometimes thought that Fallon loved the place more than she would ever love a human being. Arguing was pointless. Fallon was resigned to leaving. Andi's most creative seduction was unlikely to change Fallon's mind once she'd set it to something.

"I'll see you later tonight," Fallon said, knowing that Andi would wander into the pub and order her signature margarita, heavy on the tequila and salt, light on the syrup.

"Maybe I'll surprise you and stay home."

Fallon's eyes twinkled. Andi's husband, Dr. Jake Maguire was out of town. Her kids were away at college. There was no way that Andi would stay home. "See you later." Fallon winked and left the bedroom.

❖ ❖ ❖

"You've lost your mind."

Riley took a deep breath, willing herself not to throttle her older sister where she stood. She didn't doubt that Mary meant well. Mary always meant well. That didn't change the fact that for some reason, Mary seemed to think Riley was still a child. Riley hardly thought that a widow with a two-year-old son qualified as a child, no matter what her age on paper. She was capable of making decisions for her life without the constant input of an annoying older sister.

"Mary, please."

"Why there?"

Riley sighed. "Why not?"

"Whiskey Springs? Come on, Riley. What the hell are you going to do in Whiskey Springs, Vermont? Make cheese?"

Riley was tempted to smack her forehead. *Cheese?* She could work from anywhere. Anywhere was about to be a little town called Whiskey Springs. Robert had left her everything. That included the cabin his parents had converted to a year-round home before their passing. She needed a change, and not only a change of scenery. Riley wanted a fresh start—new beginnings.

"Do I need to remind you that you hate the country and you hate the cold?" Mary said.

Riley laughed. "I don't hate the country. The cold I could do without."

Mary stared at her sister in disbelief. No one should become a widow before the age of thirty. She had to admit; she was impressed with Riley's strength. Underneath Riley's calm exterior, Mary was sure grief and uncertainty lingered. Why Riley would decide to move three-thousand miles across the country was beyond Mary's comprehension—away from the support of family members and the familiarity of home.

"Mary," Riley sat down beside her sister. "This is what I need. If you can't understand that, at least respect it."

"What about Owen? He's two, don't you think…"

"I think that we need a change. I need the change."

"How are you going to handle being a single mom without help?"

Riley was reaching the end of her patience. She loved Mary. She appreciated all the support her sister had given her since Robert's accident. It was time she took control of her life. Robert had been gone over a year. At first, Riley wasn't sure she would survive the pain. Owen had just turned five-months-old. Life was following the course she had mapped out. She was making a living as a freelance editor and writing in her free-time, not that dealing with a baby gave her much free-time. Riley had been happy. At twenty-eight, she had been building the life she and Robert had daydreamed about since their sophomore year of college. Then it all went to hell. One drunk driver later, the present was shattered and the future had been made uncertain. She had survived. She had no choice. She had Owen. If there was one thing Riley remained grateful for it was her son. She would never be able to explain to her family that this place, the place she had envisioned making her future needed to be put in the past.

"I'll be okay," Riley replied calmly.

"You'll be alone."

Riley smiled and covered her sister's hand with hers. "Maybe that's what I need."

Mary sighed. "You can always come home. Don't forget that."

Riley nodded. *I'm not sure where home is.* She kissed Mary's cheek. "I need to get ready."

Mary watched as her little sister left the room. *Of all places —Whiskey Springs?*

Fallon chuckled as she filled two frosty mugs with beer from the tap. It never got old. She loved her job. Her mother had thought she was crazy when she quit her job in New York City and moved back to Whiskey Springs to purchase the run-down pub. She'd had her fill of the city. She'd made more money than any twenty-five-year-old had the right to. She'd landed a job at one of the largest mutual fund companies in the city after college—a job that Fallon hardly thought she was qualified to hold. She'd always had a head for numbers. She also possessed a feel for people. Her father had encouraged her to learn about the stock market in high school, and her parents had invested well for their children. Fallon had started applying her father's lessons the moment she turned eighteen, and she had made sound decisions. Three years in the city had been enough for her. She preferred the slow pace of Whiskey Springs to the bustle of Wall Street. Many of her friends had lectured her. She was giving up the golden goose. Fallon had a bright future in The Big Apple. That wasn't the future Fallon wanted. She went home. She left the city on the day before her twenty-sixth birthday and had not regretted it once.

Fallon remembered *The Middle Ground* as the little pub that sat on the outskirts of Whiskey Springs as a vibrant place where locals conversed and complained. Times were different then. Her father often took her to the pub after a day filled with fishing or sledding. He would stand at the bar and sip whiskey while she chose songs on the old jukebox in the corner. The pub had closed during her senior year of high school and had fallen into disrepair. Her father always said that everyone needed a place to unwind, to sip a strong drink, and to cast their troubles away. She loved to listen to his stories. He had found a home away from home at *The Middle Ground*. After his death, Fallon felt aimless. Something nagged at her. She'd close her eyes and see that jukebox, and she could swear she would hear her father's laughter a few feet away. The air at the bar was always thick with smoke, and Fallon recalled the fine layer of dust that always seemed to line the top of the fireplace mantle. The atmosphere at *The Middle Ground* was infinitely more appealing than some swank New York City gastropub or nightclub. And, the company? The stories told in Whiskey Springs held her interest more than the posturing she'd endured on nights out with her friends in the city. It was time to go home. That's what she did.

Fallon spent a year refurbishing the space. Everything that could go wrong seemed to go wrong. There were plumbing issues, an electrical fire threatened the entire project, and a small band of women from town had petitioned the zoning committee to deny Fallon's permits. Somehow, she'd managed to pull it off. *Murphy's Law* was born. That had been twelve years ago. Fallon had seen many of the same faces every day for the last twelve years. She knew their dreams; she'd poured away their troubles, and laughed softly at the gossip machine that churned wildly—if not accurately. *Murphy's Law* was home, so much so that she had purchased the lot of land behind the pub and built her home on it. She passed the beer mugs across the bar to a pair of familiar faces.

"Andi's here again," Dale Madigan commented.

Fallon caught Andi's gaze as she walked through the door and moved to hang up her coat.

"You know, Marge says she's been seeing that shady lawyer over there in Jericho," Pete McCann said.

"Roy Johnson?" Dale asked. "You think she's finally gonna to deep six Maguire?"

"Nah, Marge thinks she's gotten herself a boyfriend. You know Maguire. He ain't been faithful a day in his life." He shrugged. "Like Marge says, what's good for the goose is good for the gander."

Fallon snickered. *That gander's not looking for a goose.*

"What are you chuckling about there, Foster?" Dale asked. "You don't think Andi's good for an affair?"

Fallon kept her thought to herself. *Oh, she's good for an affair. She wouldn't touch Roy Johnson with your dick, Dale.* She shrugged. "Not my business."

"Yeah, but you know everyone's business." Pete held up his glass.

"Only what you fools think is *your* business *about* everyone's business," Fallon quipped.

Fallon sometimes wondered why movies always depicted women as the town gossips. They could be. The guys who sat at her bar were every bit as nosy and chatty as any woman she'd ever met, and they were far more likely to give away their secrets than any woman she'd ever served a drink. Pete and Dale were two of her regulars. Secretly, she'd deemed them Daryl and Daryl and sometimes wondered when Bob Newhart was going to make his cameo at *Murphy's Law.*

Andi made her way to the bar and offered Dale and Pete a smile. "Boys."

"Andi," Dale greeted her. "How are the boys?"

"Too busy to call their mother," she replied lightly.

Andi had two sons in college. Dave was eighteen and had started at The University of Connecticut that fall. Jacob Jr. was twenty and attended The University of Florida. They had been home for the holidays, but she had barely heard from either in weeks. She missed them. Andi also was grateful that her sons were independent and seemed to enjoy their college experience. She had cut hers short when she met their father.

Fallon had already started making Andi's drink.

"How do you know she wants that?" Pete asked Fallon. "Maybe she'd like to try something different."

Andi and Fallon's eyes locked. Andi's brow raised slightly and her eyes sparkled with mischief. Fallon felt her knees go weak. It wasn't love. Lust? It was lust in spades. She did care for Andi. Their affair had begun right after the Fourth of July. Over the months, they had become more than lovers; they were close friends—friends with some extremely enticing benefits. She supposed that she should feel some modicum of guilt. After all, Andi was a married woman. She didn't feel an iota of guilt. Jake Maguire's exploits were as well-known in Whiskey Springs as Steven Spielberg was in Hollywood. He'd been running around on Andi since before they'd married. Of course, Andi hadn't discovered that until long after her second son was born. Fallon often thought that Andi should leave the surgeon. Jake Maguire was a nice enough man. And, she had to admit that his affection for Andi was evident, as was hers for him. She'd asked Andi once why she didn't divorce Jake Maguire. Andi was an attractive woman. She could easily land a husband who would be faithful.

Fallon's finger traced a circle around Andi's breast. "Why don't you just leave him?"

Andi sighed. How could she explain this to Fallon? She loved being in Fallon's arms. She loved the way Fallon made her feel. Some part of her loved Fallon. Jake Maguire was who he was. She'd fallen in love with him twenty-six years ago and she'd loved him ever since. "I love him."

"Then why?"

"Why are we sleeping together?" Andi asked.

Fallon nodded.

Andi smiled, that bright yet solemn smile that always melted Fallon's resolve. "I need this," she confessed. "It's too hard—being alone when I know he's not."

Andi's fingertip traced Fallon's lips. Fallon was beautiful. Fallon was sweet and sincere. It would be easy to fall in love with her. Sometimes, Andi thought that she should walk away from their affair. Fallon deserved more. Fallon wasn't in love with her. Andi knew that. Fallon did care for her. She cared for Fallon. She missed Fallon when life forced them to be apart for too long. Who was she kidding? A week without Fallon's touch was torturous. Fallon touched some deep, secret part of Andi; the place where unbridled desire burned. She was free in this place. For years, she had wondered why Jake felt the need to stray. They enjoyed what Andi believed was a healthy sex life. It was gratifying. It was not adventurous. Being with Fallon in some strange way opened Andi to a new understanding. Sex with Jake was tender. It was communicative. He rocked her gently. With Fallon, Andi was rocked to her core. It wasn't the allure of their secret that made their lovemaking amazing. There was no danger to her marriage. Andi suspected that Jake knew about the affair. Her attraction to women was not a secret. After twenty-six years of marriage, few things were easy to hide. She was aware of his mistresses. He was aware of hers. They would meet in the middle.

"And," Andi continued. She looked in Fallon's bright blue eyes. "I love being with you. It's something for me, Fallon. It's just for me. It's never been to even the score. It's never been to prove anything. It's just for me. There are parts of me you will never touch, even if part of me wants you to."

Fallon smiled. Andi was referring to falling in love.

"But," Andi went on. "You touch parts of me that I will never let him see. Not because I don't trust him. It's not who we are together. It never has been."

"He was your first," Fallon guessed.

Andi smiled.

Fallon leaned in and kissed Andi softly. Her fingers drifted sensually over Andi's breast, brushing faintly across a hardening nipple. She *watched as Andi's eyes closed, anticipating where Fallon's fingers would travel next.*

Fallon felt her face flush with the memory. Somehow, she'd managed to mix Andi's margarita on auto-pilot. When Fallon came back to the present, she noticed that Andi's eyebrow had raised a degree higher. She could almost hear the laughter Andi suppressed. Andi may not have known the specific memory Fallon had drifted into; she knew it was about her.

Andi accepted her glass.

"I have no idea how you do it," Pete said to Fallon.

"What's that?" Fallon asked.

"Know what everyone wants before they ask for it," he said.

Andi licked some salt from the rim of her glass, and looked at Fallon over the top of it.

Fallon's mouth went dry. *Jesus Christ, Andi, are you trying to kill me?* She cleared her throat. "I have a good memory."

"You don't give yourself enough credit," Andi said.

Fallon's eyes opened a little wider.

Andi grinned. "It's not a skill," she said. "You have a *feel* for people."

Tingles went up and down Fallon's spine. Andi could make her wet with a few words. *She is; she's trying to kill me.* Taking a lover who was just that—a lover was thrilling in ways that Fallon had never experienced before Andi. She'd had girlfriends. She'd had one-night stands. What she shared with Andi was different. It was about more than release, but it was not about commitment. Fallon could sleep with anyone she chose at any time. And, she had on a few occasions. Those interludes had been enjoyable. Enjoyable was not exhilarating; it was, well, enjoyable. Taking a lover was titillating. The experience conjured anticipation and it allowed for exploration. She had learned how to touch Andi, how she wanted Andi to touch her, something no one-night stand could compete with. Fallon wondered what she would do if she ever met Ms. Right. Deep down, she knew that one day her time with Andi would come to an end. It would be a loss. It would hurt. It would end. For now, Fallon was resolved to savor their time together. She loved Andi's blatant flirtation that the boys never seemed to pick up on. It amused her and it aroused her.

Pete started laughing. "Oh, she's got a feel for people all right. Like that little blonde that was in here a few weeks ago. What do you use for bait?"

Fallon shook her head. Andi smiled, but Fallon could tell Pete's comment stung. It was true. Fallon had taken the woman home. Whiskey Springs sat between the shores of Lake Champlain and the ski resorts that resided close to Mt. Mansfield. There were a handful of cabins in the town that had become rental properties. And, there were always the stragglers; the drivers who got lost on some scenic route looking for moose or deer and found themselves warming by the fire at *Murphy's Law*. When Fallon had first returned to the town and opened the pub, she'd delighted in the groups of college students that found refuge by the fire. She easily related to their dialogue and their spirit of adventure. That time had long passed. Fallon was approaching her fortieth birthday. She'd be the first to admit that the cute twenty-something tourists who loved to flirt attracted her attention. She was only human. The allure of college coeds had diminished to the point of near non-existence. They tended to be inexperienced and too eager. Curiosity drove their actions; curiosity about anything they'd been told was off-limits, about the things they read in bad romance novels, and had sneaked peeks at from their parents' porn collections. As cute and sexy as many of the girls were who approached Fallon, they were just that—girls. An outwardly womanly appearance vanished when the lights dimmed and the curtains closed. All their bravado shattered. Fallon found little interest in being anyone's token lesbian experience, and she was not looking to serve as some college coed's instructor fantasy. Sure, she'd slipped a few times in the last few years. That was always after a draught that left her close to desperate for another woman's touch. She could barely recall those faces now.

"What was her name?" Dale tried to recall. "Geri or something?"

"Ginny," Fallon said.

"Right. She was cute, Foster," Dale said. "Should've invited her to stay."

Fallon was growing uncomfortable with the conversation. She kept her gaze on the two men, but she could feel Andi's eyes on her. She was accustomed to the boys' teasing and banter, not in front of her lover. Arrangements did not exile emotion. Her connection to Andi was intimate. She had an advantage in the situation. At least, she thought so. She'd been confronted with the reality of Andi's marriage and what that entailed from the beginning. Fallon never let her mind go there—to thoughts of Jake Maguire touching his wife. She knew he did. She even knew that Andi enjoyed it. They did not discuss that part of Andi's life. Andi knew Fallon had been with other women since their affair began. They did not discuss that either. Fallon never made nor accepted overtures from women in Andi's presence. She felt no desire to do so when Andi was near, and regardless of the situation there were boundaries.

"She was passing through," Fallon said.

"Aren't they all?" Pete laughed.

Andi sensed Fallon's discomfort. Her fingers caught Fallon's hand for a brief second in acknowledgment. "Oh, I don't know," Andi said. "Sooner or later one of them is going to decide to stay."

Fallon's heart skipped a beat. She looked at Andi apologetically.

Andi smiled warmly. "If you ever felt inclined to ask one of them, I'll bet they'd agree."

Fallon shook her head and chuckled. Andi's words were sincere. There had been no one that had left Fallon seeking anything more than a brief interlude except Andi, and that was different. She didn't need a relationship to be happy. If it happened, it happened. She neither sought love nor avoided it. She liked her freedom. She'd enjoyed a four-year relationship in her early thirties, and was grateful that it had resulted in a best friend, albeit a best friend that lived five-hundred miles away. Olivia Nolan had blown into Fallon's life like a tornado and left it like a leaf falling in autumn. Their courtship had been fast, furious, and passionate. Their relationship steady and supportive, and their parting not without pain, yet gentle. Fallon often thought her time with Olivia had spoiled her. Relationships carried risk. She'd had a first-row seat to the way anger and vitriol could ruin what had once been a hopeful and loving partnership. Standing behind a bar, a person learned a lot about people's lives. A few beers could open a person's emotions like a broken faucet. A few more, and their mouth tended to follow. Fallon considered herself lucky. She'd been in love. She'd enjoyed a faithful partnership, and she'd survived its end without any visible scars. In her experience, that was rare. She wasn't sure she wanted to take that gamble again. If she did, it would be with a woman unlike any she'd encountered yet, and she had encountered all kinds of women.

"Well," Fallon began. "They might stay. It doesn't mean they'll be staying with me." With that, she effectively ended the conversation.

Andi watched as Fallon busied herself with menial tasks. Fallon did that when she wanted to avoid something. The bar was quiet. Aside from the threesome at the bar, only one table enjoyed occupants. Not only was it a cold Tuesday in January; it was due to snow in a few hours. The most reserved predictions called for eight to ten inches. People had raided the grocery store, filled up their gas cans, loaded in firewood, and hunkered down. Fallon's right-hand, Carol was behind the bar. Fallon didn't even need to be at work. She chose to be here. Maybe Fallon didn't see it. Andi felt it. Fallon avoided talking about relationships. Fallon avoided entanglements. That was one of the reasons the bond Fallon and Andi shared worked. There was enormous potential in what they shared. Andi was confident they both recognized that. Had their lives taken different turns, Andi felt sure they would have made a terrific couple. Life took the turns it did, and people had to adjust to those curves. She'd made her choice and so had Fallon. There was safety in what they shared—boundaries. Occasionally, the lines seemed to bleed slightly, but neither she nor Fallon would ever let the lanes they traveled merge completely. Andi would be lying if she claimed that Fallon's desire for the single life didn't bring her a sense of relief. It also made Andi sad. Fallon was intelligent, attractive, accomplished, and most of all, she was kind—genuinely so. People gravitated to Fallon. She deserved someone that could love her completely. As much as Andi hated to think about losing what they shared, she would be happy to see Fallon in love. It would hurt—more than Andi was prepared to admit to herself. She would let Fallon go in an instant. She did love Fallon. That's how she knew she did. She wasn't in love with Fallon. She loved her, and that's why she would let her go when the time came. *I hope it does, Fallon. For your sake, I hope it does.*

CHAPTER TWO

Riley blinked rapidly, willing herself to stay awake. She'd taken her time getting to Vermont—lots of it. Traveling with a two-year-old who was potty-training meant frequent stops. It also came with constant, often indiscernible chatter. Almost two weeks, that's how long it had been since Riley had left sunny San Diego. She'd stopped in Phoenix for a night, then spent three days with a college friend in Albuquerque. It was onto Tulsa for two nights from there, where she stayed with one of Robert's cousins she hadn't seen since his funeral. It lengthened her trip, but Riley headed to Nashville next. She'd always wanted to go. It was a self-indulgent detour from the most traveled route. Two nights there helped to revitalize her. She had enjoyed being in the hotel and taking Owen for a dip at the indoor pool. From there it was off to Cleveland where her Aunt Sally lived for a two-night stint. She'd stopped in Syracuse for two more nights and had enjoyed catching up with her high-school sweetheart and his wife. Bruce and Joy had a son three-months older than Owen. She'd enjoyed watching the pair interact, and had been tempted to accept Joy's offer to stay another day or two. Weather forecasts were less than promising and Riley was determined to finish her journey. So far, she'd encountered snowy scenery, but none falling. She hated towing the small pop-up trailer behind her car. It wasn't big, but it was out of her comfort zone, and the last thing she desired was to drive with it while it snowed. She'd agreed to stay for lunch the next day. It would let her rest before the drive. Owen had been fussy, and lunch had turned into an early dinner. Now, it was eleven-thirty, dark and beginning to snow. Riley was mentally berating herself for not leaving earlier in the day when the car began to sputter.

"Just great." She glanced in the mirror at Owen. "At least one of us can sleep." The engine sputtered again and Riley felt the car buck. "Damn." She pulled over, hoping that it was the result of the cold weather. "Sure, it is." She gave it a few minutes and tried to turn the engine back over—nothing. *Stay calm.* She waited again and tried again—zip. "Shit." Riley reached for her phone—no bars. "Oh, you have got to be kidding me."

Riley huffed and shook her head. Maybe if she got out and walked a little bit she would get a signal. The sign for Whiskey Springs she had passed a short time ago read two-miles. Worst case scenario, she'd hoof it until she found civilization. She exited the warmth of the car and opened the back door. Owen groaned his protest the moment she unbuckled his seat.

"Sorry, sweetie."

Riley grabbed the diaper bag next to her son. *Better safe than sorry.* She bundled him back up tightly and put the knit cap she'd purchased in Syracuse on his head. He grumbled again.

"It's not San Diego, buddy," she said. *Trust me; this is not what I pictured doing tonight.*

She lifted Owen from his seat, closed the door, and locked the car. His arms wrapped around her neck tightly, and he let his head fall onto her shoulder. *I really hope we don't have to walk too far.* Riley took a deep breath and started forward.

❧   ❧   ❧

"Get out of here," Fallon told Carol.

"Fallon, I can close up."

"Go home," Fallon said. "I want to get the plow on the truck before I leave."

"You know, you could just hire Pete. He wouldn't charge you more than a few free beers."

Fallon shrugged. She saw no reason to hire anyone to do what she could do herself. Besides, she didn't have time to wait on other people. When the weather turned sour and most businesses closed, Fallon always managed to remain open. She'd have the lot plowed at *Murphy's Law* before dawn, and keep it clear all day. She'd open her doors when the sun was just cracking through the darkness, and serve up coffee and breakfast to the plow and tow truck drivers, cops, and the few locals who would brave the cold. One of the first things Fallon did when she opened the pub was make sure she installed a back-up generator. Combined with the fireplace at the pub's center, it provided a haven for locals when the power went out for any length of time. She enjoyed those cold winter mornings.

"No reason to hire anyone," Fallon said. "Get outta' here. Don't plan on being here tomorrow either."

"Oh, I'll get here," Carol said. "Charlie will drop me off."

"Charlie, huh?"

Carol blushed. She'd been dating Charlie Carpenter for a few months. He was the local butcher, a trade he had inherited from his father and grandfather. Charlie's family had lived in Whiskey Springs about as long as the town had existed. Depending on who you believed, that was either 1774 or 1794; seemed no one could agree on what the Town Charter's blurry writing said. Over two-hundred years of bickering hadn't solved the question. Carol had heard more than one friendly dispute erupt over the topic at *Murphy's Law*. The last time it happened, a young couple renting a cabin asked how long the town had stood. Pete and another local, Drew Johnson insisted Charlie knew the actual date. As Carol had discovered, Charlie paid little attention to the local drama whether that was who was in whose bed or when the town came into being. He had no clue and no care. Fallon had intervened.

"Don't you two know what Wikipedia is? Look it up."

Carol loved Fallon. Fallon looked out for her, and she knew that extended to the men she chose to date. "I like him," Carol admitted.

"You don't say?" Fallon laughed. "If you get bored at home with Charlie, feel free to come in. Don't worry about it, though."

"Fallon?"

"Yeah?"

"Did you think something was bothering Andi tonight?"

Fallon smiled. She suspected that more than the teasing over Fallon's sexual exploits, the mention of her boys had caused Andi's quietness. Andi missed her kids. Fallon suspected that her lover felt a bit lost without the need to play the role of mom daily in their lives. Jake traveled frequently, leaving Andi alone much of the time. For years, the boys had filled the void her husband's travels and affairs created. Now, she was alone with nothing to focus on when Jake was away. Fallon had eased Andi's loneliness. And, Andi filled a part of Fallon's life that had felt out of balance for many years. Their friendly affair gave Fallon something to look forward to aside from the pub. Fallon enjoyed their leisurely afternoons of lovemaking and long nights of sexual exploration. It was the hours they spent talking and confiding in each other that meant the most to Fallon. Those conversations always turned to Andi's kids, how much she missed them, the stories they told when they called home, and the memories it all conjured for their mother.

"I think she's missing the boys," Fallon said.

"Mm. Maybe a little disappointed that you'll be busy tonight?" Carol guessed.

Fallon sighed. She had guessed that Carol was onto the affair. This was the first mention Carol had made of any suspicion.

"Hey, it's okay," Carol said. "I get it. No one knows, Fallon. People see what they want to see."

Fallon nodded. Carol was on point. People did see what they chose to. Fallon and Carol's work gave them a different vantage point. They spent hours observing people. A great bartender could read body language. And, Carol was one of the best Fallon had ever met. Carol spent more time with Fallon than anyone. If anyone was going to figure out the dynamic between her and Andi, it would be Carol.

"I'm just saying that I think she might be missing you too —a little."

"Maybe," Fallon admitted. "How long have you known?"

"A few months," Carol confessed.

"You don't seem surprised."

"That you'd sleep with Andi? Hell, anyone with a heartbeat would sleep with her."

Fallon laughed. "Thanks, I think."

"Well, they'd sleep with you too if you gave any of them the chance."

Fallon shook her head. She made it a point not to get involved with people in town. It's not as if Whiskey Springs was exactly a lesbian smorgasbord. New York City had been far better suited to a lesbian seeking a relationship. Fallon would be the first to admit that. Plus, people liked to talk. With a population of exactly nine-hundred-ninety-nine, Whiskey Springs was small-town America personified. More than people kept secrets, their neighbors pretended to keep their secrets. Wagging tongues could cause all kinds of problems. Failed relationships and marriages were the talk of the town, making it difficult to maintain friendships and privacy. The conversation might've been kept to whispering in quiet corners. It didn't take long for the whispering to weave its way from nosy neighbors to busy-body church ladies to curious shop owners and back to the source again. Often, the story had changed so much by that point that the perpetrator didn't recognize it, and it all began again. She'd come to understand that there were two kinds of gossip: curious chatter and rabid rumors. Curious chatter was a bi-product of being human. As her mother always said, people were naturally curious. That didn't make them small-minded as some might suggest; it made them human. Rabid rumors were the result of something sinister—an objective to smear a person's reputation for personal gain. Fortunately, Fallon had only encountered the latter a handful of times in Whiskey Springs. Nonetheless, knowing that your life or relationship was the chosen topic of conversation at the pub, the market, the butcher, the hairdresser, and at church coffees was not inclined to make a person feel welcome.

Whiskey Springs had neither grown by leaps and bounds nor had it diminished in size over the years. Fallon thought she understood the reason why. Many people left for college, started their career elsewhere, met their significant other, and then moved back to the town after they were better established. One would have thought that dynamic would lead to rapid growth. When relationships went awry, when older children found themselves in some trouble, or a marriage ended in divorce, some or all parties tended to leave the town. The move might be as simple as a few miles away or as far as across the country. When a couple divorced, if one left for different parts, chatter tended to move from constant rumbling to sympathetic outreach. Small town life like big city living had its ups and downs. Understanding how the community worked had shaped much of Fallon's perspective on pursuing relationships. She had no intention of leaving her home, and that left her cautious when it came to romantic involvement.

There was no one in Whiskey Springs that Fallon had any desire to pursue besides Andi. Who would she date; Daryl and Daryl? As much as she loved a pair of warm flannel pajamas, the likes of Pete and Dale were not enticing to her—wrong style, wrong interests, and most of all wrong parts. Andi held her interest, and not just in the bedroom. And, being with Andi was safe. The fact was, even if anyone suspected that Andi was sleeping with her, no one was likely to utter a word. People felt for Andi. She was a kind, beautiful, outgoing woman who had lived nearly her entire life in the town. Everyone knew about Jake Maguire's lifestyle. That had been humiliating for Andi. Andi had always held her head high. She'd resisted becoming a jaded woman. People felt for her. No one suspected Andi's attraction to women, of that Fallon was sure. And, few people were likely to make waves for Fallon, not because of the pub or who she was—but because of her mother.

Ida Foster was no less than an icon in the town. She'd been a school-teacher turned principal turned mayor, an office she'd held until two years ago. Fallon's mother was born and raised in Whiskey Springs as was her father, and four generations before him. Ida had always been known as a compassionate, loving, God-fearing, and honest woman. When Fallon had first moved back home, a few people took issue with her efforts to resurrect the pub that stood on the edge of town. At first, Ida had laughed it off as a handful of ladies hoping to revive prohibition. When word traveled back to her that the plot to derail Fallon stemmed from offense over Fallon's sexuality, the town got to view a different side to Ida Foster. Nothing was more dangerous that a mama bear protecting her cub. Fallon would have thought people here would've learned that lesson long ago. Occasionally, people needed a reminder. No one had taken issue with Fallon since, at least, not outside of tight-knit circles around a kitchen table.

"Well, now that Charlie's off the market unless Daryl and Daryl undergo some metamorphosis and become Venus and Serena, I'll pass."

Carol laughed. "Okay, I get it—back off."

"No, I just…"

"Don't say anything else. Are you sure you don't want me to close up shop? It would give you the time to pop over to Andi's before you have to plow?"

"I'm sure," Fallon said. She was tempted to accept. Their morning together had been amazing, and Fallon imagined it would be days if not a week before she would meet Andi again privately. If she went to meet Andi, she'd be gone until the wee hours. There would be no chance for rest, and Fallon needed some.

Carol wrapped Fallon in a hug. "Just don't hurt yourself."

"Never gonna' live that down." Last December, Fallon had nearly cut off a finger trying to hitch the plow to her truck. It was a freak accident, a slip that caused her finger to get caught. The boys had never let it go.

Carol winked. "I'll see you tomorrow."

Fallon stepped back inside and behind the bar. She was tempted to pour herself a drink. Knowing that the next day was likely to start in a few hours or less, she thought better of the idea and put on a pot of coffee instead. She looked down at her phone and chuckled.

Andi: You're really going to make me take care of this myself?

Fallon typed in her response.

Fallon: You know, the roads are slick already.

Andi: It's not just the roads that are wet, Fallon.

Fallon laughed. "You are going to kill me one of these days."

Fallon: Let me know when it starts sticking and I'll come dig you out.

Andi: Cute.

Fallon startled when her phone rang. "Yes?"

"What are you doing?" Andi asked.

"What are *you* doing?"

"Thinking about what I wish you were doing."

"Is that right?"

Andi sighed. "Might not see you for a week or so."

"I know."

"That's a long time," Andi breathed.

Fallon sat down on a bar stool. It wasn't the first time she'd listened or watched as Andi touched herself. She'd like to say that watching was more of a turn-on, but there was something intensely arousing about hearing Andi and not being able to see her. It reminded Fallon of her youth, all the nights she would close her bedroom door and imagine Andi naked—imagine touching Andi while she explored herself. Andi might not realize it, but she'd taught Fallon a great deal about pleasure before they'd ever slept together. Fantasies of Andi Sherman drove Fallon to learn how she liked to be touched, and she had no doubt that those nights had made her a more adept lover. Now, she could picture Andi clearly. She didn't need to conjure a fantasy. She'd memorized the expression on Andi's face as Andi hovered close to climax. She'd felt Andi's heart race and heard her whimpers gradually change to strangled cries of ecstasy. She could hear Andi's uneven breathing on the phone. It made her heart beat slightly out of time. *Maybe, I should've taken Carol up on her offer.* She bit her lip gently as she listened to her lover.

"Too long," Andi said.

"Oh?" Fallon played along. "What would I be doing if I were there?"

"You'd be inside me."

A jolt traveled from Fallon's ears straight to her center. *Jesus.* On second thought, maybe this was better than being there. *No way.*

"You'd be licking me," Andi said.

"Yeah? Is that what you are imagining right now? Me between your thighs?"

Andi gasped.

"You are," Fallon surmised. *If only you knew how many times I imagined that over the years.* "Tell me. What do I feel like?"

"Warm," Andi breathed. "Wet… Soft…"

Warm and wet were excellent ways to describe Fallon's current physical state as well. Had she not been in front of two large windows, Fallon would have become more than a verbal participant in their play. These were the parts of Andi that Jake had never and would never share—Andi's unbridled desire. Fallon loved it.

"You want me to make you come?" Fallon asked.

Andi groaned. "Yes," she hissed.

"Umm. You want to imagine it's my tongue playing with you right now instead of your fingers."

"Yes."

"Soft and slow, Andi. Take it soft and slow. Not yet. You like it when I tease you." *Jesus, who is getting more out of this?* Fallon steadied her breathing. She heard Andi's breath catch and sputter. "Not yet."

"Please."

"You want to beg me?"

Andi moaned. "Yes."

"Slow down," Fallon instructed. "Easy. Soft, just like I touched you before I left this morning."

Andi gasped. "Fallon…"

Fallon was losing her resolve. The temptation to plunge her hand into her jeans was growing by the second. She closed her eyes. She could almost feel Andi's hands in her hair. *God help me.* "Now," Fallon said. "Come on baby, right now. Feel me right now."

Andi screamed, announcing her pleasure. "Make me come, Fallon! Oh… Baby…"

Fallon throbbed with desire. Every inch of her begged to be touched. Her body screamed at her to relieve the ache—right now. She closed her eyes and groaned.

"I wish you were here," Andi whispered.

"You have no idea how much I want to be."

"I'll miss you."

"Mm."

Andi giggled. "Frustrated?"

"You have no idea."

"Take care of it," Andi suggested.

Jesus. "I wish I could." *Trust me, when I get home later, I will.*
She sighed. "You are sexy as hell; you know that?"

"You might be a tad biased."

"No," Fallon said honestly. "You are."

Andi rolled over and hugged the pillow Fallon had rested
on earlier that day. "I'll miss you, Fallon." It was the truth. She
would.

"You'll see me," Fallon reminded her. She heard Andi sigh.
"I'll miss you too."

"Be careful out there, Fallon."

"I won't cut off any appendages you find useful," Fallon
teased.

"I'm serious."

"I'll be careful."

"Text me when you finish," Andi requested.

"Finish with plowing or finish relieving this pain you've
inflicted?"

Andi grinned. "You can call me for that too."

Fallon chuckled. "Get some rest."

"Text me, Fallon."

"I promise." Fallon took a deep breath and placed her
phone on the counter. She smiled. Andi was one of a kind. She
blew out her breath and started for the coffee maker when
something caught her eye outside the window. "What the
hell…"

❧ ❧ ❧

Riley's legs were growing tired. She couldn't imagine how
Owen had managed to stay asleep. She'd nearly dropped him
twice. She jostled him on her shoulder and looked at her
phone. A black screen met her gaze. "Fuck me." She tried to
power the phone on—no luck. "This is ridiculous. It can't be
much further." She'd been repeating that mantra for what felt
like hours. She was cold, tired, and nervous. There were no

street lights. As the snow began to fall steadily, she feared she might lose her bearings. What could she do? She couldn't sleep on the side of the road with Owen. It wasn't safe. She strained to make out something in the distance. Up ahead, she could faintly make out what looked to be some neon signs in a window. "Civilization, buddy," she whispered to her son. "Thank God."

Riley pressed ahead, willing her legs to keep carrying her weight and Owen's. Finding light was promising, but she suspected she had farther to travel than it appeared. Frankly, another two steps seemed too far to traverse. She tightened her hold on Owen and offered a silent prayer to anyone who might be listening. *Please, just let me get there.*

Fallon moved to look out the window. "What…" She squinted to bring an approaching figure into focus. "What on earth?"

Fallon grabbed her jacket and flew out the front door of *Murphy's Law.* As the figure came into clearer focus, Fallon's pace increased. "Hey!" She called out.

"Oh, thank God." Riley stumbled slightly.

Fallon caught the young woman. "Are you okay?"

"I don't know. We've been walking a while."

Fallon's gaze narrowed with concern.

"My car," Riley's thoughts seemed to spin in time with her head. "My phone…"

Fallon caught her again. "Whoa… Let's get you inside."

"Inside?" Riley asked.

Fallon pointed to the building behind her. The young woman seemed confused. Her legs wavered. Fallon put an arm around her and guided her toward the pub. "Let's get you inside and warmed up, and we'll figure out how you ended up here." *Good thing I didn't head to Andi's.* She opened the door to the pub and helped her charge inside.

"Where are we?" Riley asked.

Fallon almost laughed at the irony. If nothing else, the pub was aptly named. "Welcome to Murphy's Law," she said as she offered the woman a chair. Fallon knelt in front of her. "Let's try this again now that we're someplace a little warmer." She smiled. "I'm Fallon," she said. "This is my pub, Murphy's Law."

Riley nodded. "Riley," she introduced herself.

"And, who is this?" Fallon inquired.

Owen's eyes had begun to open. He reached for the hat on his head and discarded it. Fallon chuckled. *Typical.*

"This is Owen," Riley explained. She took the first deep breath she had since leaving the car on the side of the road. "My car," she began again. "I don't know what happened. It started bucking. I pulled over and it just…"

"Died?" Fallon guessed

Riley nodded. "I didn't have any cell service."

"So, you thought you'd walk until you got some."

Riley nodded again.

"Umm. That can be tricky out here sometimes," Fallon said. She studied Riley thoughtfully for a minute. "How about a cup of coffee to warm up?"

"I'm sorry. Do you have a phone I could use? I can have someone tow…"

"You're not going to get anybody out here now," Fallon said. "Not for a few hours. By then the snow will be coming down full-speed. Cream or sugar?"

"Both."

Fallon handed Riley a mug of coffee. "Any idea where the car is?" Fallon asked.

"I'd just passed a sign for Whiskey Springs. It said two miles."

That's a good mile down the road. "You were walking a while. Where are you heading?"

Riley sipped her coffee carefully as Owen fidgeted on her lap. "Home." *Whatever that means.*

Fallon was curious. "Where's home?"

"It's supposed to be 22 River Drive in Whiskey Springs."

"The Main's place?"

Riley nodded. "You know it?"

"I ought to. I spent plenty of time there when I was a kid."

Riley shook her head. "I don't understand."

"My mother and Sylvia Main are friends."

"Sylvia is my husband's grandmother. Well, she was his… He's no longer…"

Fallon nodded. "I heard. I'm sorry."

"You heard?"

"Small town," Fallon said. "My mother mentioned someone was taking over the place." Owen chose that moment to protest his mother's grasp. Fallon managed to catch him before he hit the floor. "Easy there, buddy."

Riley set down her mug and took custody of her son again. "I know you're tired," she cooed to him. "Hang in there for a few minutes." She kissed his head. *Like that will work.*

"Look," Fallon began cautiously. "What kind of car do you have?"

Riley's confusion was evident.

"I can probably tow it with my truck. If I don't get a move on, it's likely to get plowed in when they start clearing the roads."

"Shit," Riley muttered.

Fallon grinned.

"It's a Ford Explorer, but there's a small cargo trailer attached that…"

"I understand. Shouldn't be an issue." *Shit. I'll probably have to make two trips.*

"Listen, I don't want to put you out. You don't even know me…"

"No offense, I don't think you have many choices," Fallon said honestly. She glanced out the window. *And, you're probably not going to like what I am about to say.* "It's already after midnight. In another hour or two it's going to be a complete white-out. I could try to get you to your house. If I do, I'll lose the window to tow the car."

Riley sighed. *Great. What am I going to do? Sleep in a bar with a toddler?*

Fallon sensed Riley's unease. "Look, I know that you don't know me from Adam. I get that. I've lived here most of my life. I know these roads and how they'll look shortly." She took a deep breath. "My house is up the hill right behind where we are. I can take you and your son up there while I tow the car and trailer here…"

"I can't ask you…"

"You didn't. He looks like he needs a bed, and frankly so do you."

"Gee thanks."

Fallon shrugged. "It's understandable," she said. "If it helps, my mom was the mayor for almost twenty-years. She'd kill me if I didn't help you out. The fact that you're related to Sylvia? Well, there's no coming back from that."

"You're Ida Foster's daughter?"

"Unfortunately for her at times," Fallon joked. "Let me guess; Sylvia told you to look her up."

"Yeah, something like that."

"Listen, Riley, I really don't think either of us has much choice here. I've got the room. You've got a toddler, and we've got a storm rolling in."

Riley wasn't certain if she wanted to scream, cry, or hug Fallon. Fallon's words made sense. Still, she didn't know this woman at all. What was she supposed to do?

"I know it probably doesn't mean much—my promise that is. I promise you will be safe—if that helps at all."

"I could just wait here and…"

"You can. If that's what you are comfortable with, you can. There's heat and you are welcome to call anyone you like. Like I said, I live up the hill. I'll have to be down here to plow the lot later anyway. If you want to stay here, that's fine. It's a lot more comfortable up there. Trust me on that. I should know. You can get some rest. I'll make sure your car gets to the garage tomorrow and we'll get you home. I'm sure Pete has a loaner you can borrow at the shop until he works things out with your car."

Riley's head was spinning again. Pete? Who the hell was Pete? Why would anyone offer to let a stranger stay in her home? What was the catch? Maybe she'd hit her head and landed in Oz or something. Owen began to groan and kick. He was exhausted. She was freezing *and* exhausted. What else could she do?

"My place is nicer than this," Fallon tried to lighten the mood. "Come on. I'll drive you up there."

Riley nodded dumbly. If nothing else, she would have a story to tell. "Fallon?"

"Yeah?"

"I…"

"Don't sweat it."

❧ ❧ ❧

Fallon was eager to get Riley Main settled so that she could get moving on her tasks. The snow seemed to be falling faster each second. *So much for rest.* Despite her frustration, her heart went out to Riley. It was obvious that Riley felt both anxious and guilty. Anxious Fallon could easily understand. Guilty? What was that saying? Shit happens. She led Riley to her bedroom. "You two can have this room. There's a bathroom if you want to take a shower. Plenty of towels in the closet in there." Fallon reached in a drawer and pulled out some sweatpants and a thermal shirt. "Probably too big for you, but they're warm and dry," Fallon said.

"I can't accept…"

"Hey, what do they say?"

Riley shook her head.

"Shit happens?" Fallon winked. "Make the best of it."

"What about you?"

"Me? I'm going to go get your car and that trailer off the side of the road. Then I'm going to plow the lot and then I'll crash on the sofa like I always do. Seriously, don't worry about it."

"I'm going to owe you…"

"You don't owe me anything," Fallon said honestly. "I'm glad I was still at the pub."

"Me too."

"Everything here is pretty self-explanatory. Just help yourself. I'll be back as soon as I can."

"Fallon, I'm sorry about…"

"If anyone should apologize, it's me."

"What?"

"I usually spring for dinner before I invite a woman into my bedroom." Fallon winked and left Riley in her bedroom with Owen.

Riley laughed and placed Owen on the bed and started to undress him. "We got lucky, little man." *What a beginning.* Owen giggled. "You think so too, huh? We're going to have to find some way to thank Fallon." Owen grinned. "I agree. She's a nice person." *Well, there is that. If everyone is that nice here, we might just do okay.* "All right, little man. I think we've both had enough excitement for one day."

❧ ❧ ❧

Fallon flipped on her high-beams and headed down the road. The night had gone in a completely different direction than she had expected. She couldn't imagine how Riley must be feeling. She was curious about the young woman. Her mother had mentioned that Sylvia's granddaughter-in-law was making her way from the West Coast to Whiskey Springs. Ida and Sylvia Main had been friends almost since birth. Fallon remembered the tears in her mother's eyes when Sylvia and her husband, Frank left for Florida. Frank had suffered with respiratory issues and the after-effects of a minor stroke. They had left for the sunshine state just a month after Fallon's father's untimely death. Fallon had been in New York, her brother, Dean was stationed with the Navy in Norfolk, Virginia. Ida did her best to conceal her loneliness from Fallon. If Fallon felt adrift, she couldn't imagine how her mother felt. It helped solidify Fallon's decision to come home.

Ida had confided to Fallon that she hoped Sylvia might return to Whiskey Springs. That had yet to occur. The year after Fallon's father's death, Frank Main suffered a major heart attack and died. Less than six months later, Sylvia's son Dan, and his wife Rebecca were killed in a car accident. Fallon had thought Sylvia might find her way home after that. She had stayed. Her grandchildren were still in school and she now had them in her care. Fallon could hardly believe it when her mother told her that Sylvia's oldest grandson had met the same fate as his parents. *Poor Sylvia.* Losing her father had sent Fallon into depression for months. The idea of losing so many people you loved seemed unfathomable. And, Riley? Riley couldn't be much over thirty—if that. Here she was a single mom and a widow already. Fallon shook her head. *That sucks.* Now, she found herself stranded in some stranger's house all the way across the country. *Poor Riley.*

Fallon leaned forward and wiped the wind shield with her hand. "There you are." She turned the truck around and backed up toward Riley's car. The snow was beginning to accumulate at a rate that concerned Fallon. She would need to work fast if she hoped to get both the car and the trailer to the parking lot at the pub. As it was, she would be behind in her endeavor to clear the lot. She let out a groan when the cold air hit her face. *What else can go wrong tonight?*

❧   ❧   ❧

Riley tossed and turned on the bed. Owen had fallen asleep the moment she covered him. "I envy you, little man." She kissed her son's head. Riley's thoughts were spinning out of control. How had she landed here? Landed in some stranger's home? In some stranger's bed? Riley chuckled. *Like that would ever happen.* She sighed with frustration. "What am I doing?" That was a stupid question. She was doing the only thing she could do, and not just because her car died at the side of a country road. She needed a change. She needed a fresh start. This was not what she had envisioned. What had she envisioned? Riley tossed some more.

A breakdown in San Diego would have resulted in a tow truck and a ride home from Mary or any number of friends. *Maybe I should've tried clicking my heels three times.* She had to laugh. Robert would have found Riley's current predicament amusing. She was certain of that. He would have seen it as an adventure. Then again, Robert tended to see everything as an adventure. *I miss you.* Becoming a widow at twenty-eight was not in Riley's life plan. Finding herself in a Podunk, New England town lying in a woman's bed she'd met in front of a bar with her two-year-old shouldn't have seemed all that strange. She shook her head. *Only you, Riley.*

How long had she been lying here? Riley grabbed her phone from the bedside table. Fallon had explained that the phone's sudden death was likely the result of the cold. She'd pointed out the charger before leaving. Then again, Fallon had pointed out almost everything in a matter of minutes. She'd made certain that Riley knew where everything she might need was. She'd handed Riley warm clothes, and tried with everything she had to make Riley feel comfortable in an inherently uncomfortable situation. Just who was Fallon Foster? Riley looked at the time on her phone. How had it gotten to be three in the morning? Where was Fallon? Riley felt a lump grow in her throat. What if something happened while Fallon was trying to help her? *I hope she's okay.*

Fallon was tempted to punch something. She'd managed to get Riley's car moved to the parking lot. Towing the trailer was proving a more challenging task. For the third time, Fallon found herself exiting her truck to see if she could free the trailer's wheels from the icy mixture on the ground. "Two o'clock already? Shit." Fallon pulled off a glove and dug some ice out from under a wheel. "Now, behave! It's only a little way up the road. Don't make me tell you again!" Fallon made her way back to the driver's seat. Determined to make it the last quarter of a mile to the pub's lot, Fallon punched the gas harder than normal. *Come on.*

"Thank God," Fallon muttered as she pulled into the parking lot. She pulled the trailer even with Riley's car. "One task done." Fallon looked at the lot and shook her head. There had to be at least five inches on the ground. Now, she would need to fasten the plow to the front of her truck. She'd never get up the hill to her house without it. And, the lot? That would take time to clear. *Probably close to an hour. Dammit. So much for sleep.* She made her decision and lifted the phone from her pocket.

"Foster?"

"Yeah, figured you'd be getting up about now."

"Yeah. You know the drill. Winter's my bread and butter," Pete replied.

"So, how'd you like a little extra butter on that bread?" Fallon asked.

"You got a lead for me?"

"Yeah, my parking lot, a tow job, and replacing what I suspect is a bad fuel pump."

Pete was stunned. He rubbed his eyes. "Your truck died?"

"No, not mine. I'll explain later. I'm about to give the lot a once over, but if you could hit it again in a couple of hours so I can get a little rest…."

"You gonna open in the morning?" Pete asked.

"I hope so."

"Whatever you need," he said. "You okay, Fallon? You sound kind of strange."

"Tired." Fallon was tired. The strangeness Pete heard in her voice stemmed more from her discomfort with asking for help. It wasn't that she doubted Pete's willingness to help. He'd made the offer to take care of plowing for Fallon for years. Fallon simply prided herself on being self-sufficient. She preferred to be the helper rather than the person seeking assistance. "Look, I'm sorry to have to ask…"

"Seriously?" Pete laughed. "Just give me an open tab."

Fallon laughed. "I'll make sure you get more than that."

"I'll be there around five."

"Thanks, Pete." Fallon shoved the phone back into her pocket. She stepped back into the cold and readied the plow. "Let's hope I don't injure anything important." She snickered. *Andi will kill me.* That thought brought a smile to Fallon's lips. She was not looking forward to a week without Andi's company. She did know it'd be worth the wait. *No injuries, Foster. I just hope I thaw out by then.*

CHAPTER THREE

Fallon walked into the house and shook the snow from her hair.

"No hat?"

Fallon turned to the sound of Riley's voice. She'd tried to be quiet when she pulled in the driveway. She imagined the sound of the plow coming up the hill had awakened her visitor. "I'm sorry," Fallon apologized.

"You should be," Riley replied seriously.

Fallon's eyes popped wider.

"It's freezing out there. No hat? You're worse than Owen."

Riley's triumphant grin told Fallon she was pleased with herself. "You sound like my mom," Fallon said. She hung up her coat and kicked off her boots. "I am sorry. I didn't mean to wake you."

"You didn't."

Fallon sensed Riley's lingering unease.

"You're shivering," Riley noted. "I should probably let you get warm and get some sleep."

"I won't be able to sleep yet. How do you feel about a toddy?" Fallon asked.

Riley's perplexed glance made Fallon laugh.

"I'll assume that's a new word in your vocabulary."

"No. Isn't that Whiskey in tea or something?"

"Bourbon if you'd prefer."

Riley shuddered.

"Still don't trust me, huh?" Fallon teased.

"I... it's not…"

Fallon laughed. "Don't knock it 'til you've tried it."

Riley shivered slightly.

"Still cold?" Fallon asked. "Never mind, I know the answer."

"You must think I'm a wimp," Riley said.

"I think you're cold."

"You just came in from out there," Riley pointed to the door.

"I'm used to it," Fallon said. "You're not. I take it Owen is sleeping?"

"Out like a light the moment his head hit the pillow."

Fallon led Riley into the living room. She grabbed a blanket from the back of the sofa, draped it around Riley's shoulders and guided her to sit.

"Have a seat," Fallon said. She moved to the fireplace.

"What are you doing?"

"Hopefully, warming you up."

"You don't have to..."

Fallon was already moving logs and kindling to the fireplace. She frequently failed to make it to bed, choosing to recline in her chair or stretch out on the sofa in front of the fire. As the fire would dwindle to embers, so would Fallon slip into sleep. In moments, a small fire had begun to crackle.

"It'll heat up quickly," Fallon said. "Just relax here."

"Where are you going?"

"Toddies, remember?"

Riley grimaced.

Fallon offered her a wink and set off to complete her task.

Riley watched Fallon go and sighed, wondering again how she ended up here. Why was she complaining? *Poor Fallon.* It was after three in the morning. Fallon had been up half the night, largely, Riley was sure because of Riley's plight. She should've left Syracuse earlier. Who was she kidding? Maybe

Mary was right; maybe she should have stayed in San Diego. She hadn't even reached her new home and things were a mess. She was inconveniencing a stranger. What would she have done without Fallon? The situation unnerved her. She shivered. What was wrong with her? She'd dressed Owen in a clean sleeper and he'd fallen asleep contentedly in Fallon's bed. Snug as a bug in a rug, as the saying went. Riley couldn't seem to get warm to save her life. If only Fallon's remedy would do the trick.

Her stomach roiled at the thought of whiskey in tea. She shuddered again, unsure if her body was reacting to the thought of Fallon's concoction or if was a result of the cold she seemed to feel down to her bones. The fire was beginning to grow from a crackle to a roar. She felt its heat reach her cheeks and closed her eyes. Maybe, finally, she could shake this chill.

"A little better?" Fallon asked. She handed Riley a mug full of steaming liquid.

"I don't know." Riley sniffed the contents of the mug. "I thought I was."

Fallon chuckled. "Just try it. Perfect remedy."

"I thought these were for a cold not for *being* cold."

"Yeah, well, I know they say the two don't go hand in hand. Can't prove that by me. You get too cold, you get a cold. Give it a try," Fallon said.

Riley tentatively took a sip.

Fallon watched with amusement as Riley considered the taste and scent of her drink.

"It tastes like honey," Riley said.

"I might've gone heavy on the sweet and light on the Whiskey," Fallon confessed.

"Fallon, I really appreciate everything you've done for me. You don't know me at all…"

"I know you are from San Diego, you are Sylvia's grand-daughter, well in-law or whatever, you have a son, your car is dead in my parking lot, and you are definitely not used to the cold. What else do I need to know?" Fallon asked.

"When you put it that way. I am sorry if I've caused any…"

"You really like to apologize, don't you?"

"Sorry."

Fallon raised her brow.

Riley giggled. For some reason, Fallon put her at ease.

Fallon sipped her tea and closed her eyes. The warmth of the fire relaxed her.

"You must be exhausted," Riley said.

"Right now, I'm relaxed. The fire does that for me." Fallon opened her eyes. "By the way, pretty sure your fuel pump is bad."

Riley opened her mouth to speak but Fallon continued before she had the chance.

"Can't say for sure, but I'd bet a few bucks that's the culprit. Pete will tow it over to his place later today. Hopefully, before he makes full use of his open tab." She chuckled.

"Pete?"

"Oh, I keep forgetting—Pete owns the local garage. He's kind of a fixture at Murphy's."

"Oh."

"He'll fix her up good as new," Fallon promised. "Once Carol gets in tomorrow, I can tow the trailer to your place and drop you off."

"Carol?"

"She runs the pub." Fallon laughed. "Everyone thinks that's me. Nope. I pay the bills and pour some drinks. She's the one who makes it all work."

Riley's head had entered its millionth spin of the night. Fallon spoke as if they were old friends. And, somehow it felt that way. The entire scene made Riley curious about who Fallon Foster was. One thing she did feel certain of; Fallon likely could handle anything.

"How long have you owned the pub?" Riley asked.

"Oh, about fourteen years now."

Riley was surprised. Fallon appeared to be in her thirties.

"I'll take that look as a complement. I bought it when I was twenty-six. It took me a year to get it open."

Riley was curious.

"It used to be called *The Middle Ground*. I think because it's on the edge of Whiskey Springs, heading toward Underhill. Anyway, it closed when I was in high school."

"And, you always wanted to own it?"

Fallon laughed. "Nope. Never gave it much thought until my dad died."

"I'm sorry."

Fallon shrugged. "Thanks. It's okay. It was unexpected. I guess it made me rethink a lot of things."

"I understand."

"Shit, I'm sorry, Riley. I didn't mean to bring up…"

"It's okay," Riley said. It was okay. Riley was enjoying getting to know Fallon, even if it was in the middle of the night under crazy circumstances. People tended to walk on egg shells around Riley. They were hesitant to talk about loss or death. At first, she appreciated the space. Now, it frustrated her. Loss was part of life. It was impossible to avoid the topic. It was difficult to get to know anyone when everyone felt the need to protect her. "I do understand. Please, I want to hear the story." She did.

Fallon nodded. "I guess you would get it. I don't know. It's like everything made sense until that day. Then he was gone, and all of a sudden, all my plans seemed like they were someone else's—like I'd missed something important."

Oh, I understand.

"Every time I thought about him, I thought about that pub. He would take me there with him after we went fishing or sledding, really any excuse he could find to pop in and see his friends." She chuckled. "I liked to play the jukebox, and drinking the Shirley Temples. They came with a cherry."

Riley smiled. Fallon's eyes brightened like a child's on Christmas morning as she spoke. She had noticed the jukebox in the corner of the pub when Fallon led her inside. *It all comes together.*

"Anyway, everyone thought I was crazy—when I moved home and bought the place, I mean."

"Moved home?"

"Oh, yeah. I keep forgetting—you don't know any of this." Fallon chuckled. She did keep forgetting. She barely knew Riley. For some unknown reason, she felt inclined to share her entire life with her guest. She was accustomed to being surrounded by people who knew her history. "This is probably boring…"

"Not at all," Riley said. Fallon was refreshing. "Please."

"Well… I was living in the city at the time." Fallon saw Riley's unspoken question. "New York," she clarified.

Riley nodded.

"I had this great job, at least, everyone else thought so."

"You didn't?"

Fallon shrugged. "For a little while, I guess I did. I made a lot of money." Fallon chuckled. *More money than I had a right to.* "It was okay. It just didn't feel like home, I guess."

Riley related to that feeling. Before Robert's death, she'd felt content with her life in San Diego. After he was gone, everything felt out of place. She'd waited, given it time to fall back into order. It never had. Something nagged at her. It wasn't just Robert's absence that made her feel out of balance. She wasn't sure what drove her feelings. San Diego wasn't *home.* It was a place. She had friends who loved her—friends she loved. That did little to ease her distress. She'd considered a million possibilities. Her mother had invited her to move to Seattle. She could sell the house and buy a new one. It was Sylvia's suggestion that Riley give Whiskey Springs a try that seemed to haunt her. The idea tugged at something deep within her. Robert had shared fond memories of the town. She had never visited. It had been too much for him after his parents' deaths. He kept putting off a visit. It made no sense that Riley felt inclined to traverse the entire country to give life in Vermont a try. The thought wouldn't leave her alone. Eventually, she gave in.

"It happens," Riley offered. "So, you came home?"

Fallon sipped her tea. "How do you like it?" She briefly changed the subject and gestured to the mug in Riley's hands.

"Not bad," Riley admitted. "And warm."

"Told you." Fallon sighed. "Are you sure you want to hear this? You must be tired."

Riley was sure that when she did crash it would be for hours. Exhaustion was a strange thing sometimes. Her body was tired, but her brain was nowhere close to turning off. "I don't think my brain is listening to the rest of me," she said.

"I get that."

"Finish your story. I'm curious about Murphy's Law."

"Anything that can go wrong, will go wrong?" Fallon laughed. "Believe me; the name fits."

"I take it there were some issues."

"Understatement. Aside from the fact that my mother was ready to have me committed? Let's see, there was Mary Brannigan and Dora Bath. I like to call them B squared."

Riley chuckled.

"And, not because of their last names."

"Yeah, I kind of figured that," Riley said.

"Dick Bath—and before you say it, I know how bad that sounds."

Riley coughed. "Did his parents hate him?"

"I don't know. Pretty sure Dora does, though."

Riley shook her head. Fallon's story had only begun and Riley was both amused and intrigued. "So, what's the deal with Dick Bath?" She choked slightly again. "That sounds *awful*."

"Right?" Fallon laughed. She would never understand why the man didn't choose to go by Frank or Fran, Francis—anything but Dick. Dick Bath? It was horrendous. "He's the zoning commissioner. Which in Whiskey Springs is about as thrilling as being a safari guide in New York City."

"Lots of work, I take it?"

"Exactly. Anyway, B squared did not want me to open the pub. I don't think they wanted *me* to open up any kind of shop here."

"Why not?"

"Oh, well," Fallon took a breath. "At first, I thought it was the idea that the boys would have a place to gather again, like the pub was a threat to their marriages or yard work or something. Turned out it had more to do with the fact they thought I might be some kind of threat to their daughters."

Riley smiled, immediately catching Fallon's meaning. "Not a lot of lesbian bars in Whiskey Springs."

"Not a one. Not a lot of lesbians either," Fallon said. "Well, maybe one." She winked.

"What did they think—you were trying to colonize or something?"

Fallon's burst of laughter took them both off guard. "Sorry. It's a tempting prospect."

Riley smirked. She didn't need to explore Whiskey Springs in the light to know that it was a small town that lacked the diversity of San Diego or New York City. "So, you get to be the token lesbian who owns the token bar? That must've made you the town hero."

"It's a tough job."

"I'll bet. So, they obviously didn't succeed."

"Not once my mother got wind."

"Oh, Mama Bear."

"Um-hum. The thing about my mom is she loves everybody, but she won't hesitate to give anyone a dose of the truth."

"Especially when it comes to you."

"Or my brother."

"So, you survived B squared."

"Only to have an electrical fire, a flood, and a tree put a hole in the roof."

"No..."

"I swear. Understand the name now?" Fallon asked.

"Did you ever want to quit?"

"Every day for a year," Fallon admitted. "I just kept picturing the jukebox. I don't know; I could hear my dad's voice. I'm glad I kept going. Best decision I ever made."

"That has to feel good."

"Most of the time," Fallon said.

"Do you miss the city?" Riley wondered.

"Sometimes. I can always visit." She could always visit her friends in the city. She rarely did. They visited her under the pretense of a ski weekend or a week at the lake.

Riley yawned.

Fallon got up from her chair and plucked the mug from Riley's hand. "You should try and get a little sleep."

"What about you?" Riley yawned again. "I can grab Owen and..."

"No," Fallon put Riley's thought to rest. "I have to head down to the pub in about an hour."

Riley was stunned. "Fallon, you haven't slept at all."

"I'll sleep later. Really, I'm okay." Fallon smiled at the genuine concern in Riley's eyes. Perhaps there was a silver-lining to the chaos of the night for them both. Fallon sensed a budding friendship, something she would welcome. "Get some sleep," she told Riley. "Give me a call when you wake up and I'll bring you down to the pub for breakfast."

"Breakfast?"

"Yeah. I try to open for the guys by six or so. Coffee and breakfast. There isn't any other place for them to stop except a gas station, so..."

Riley smiled. *Who are you, the pied piper?* "On one condition."

"There are conditions?"

"Yeah. You let me repay the favor and make you dinner some night. I'll probably need to find filet mignon to call it even…"

"I have an in with the local butcher."

Riley laughed. *Of course, you do.* She started for the bedroom and turned back. "Fallon?"

"Yeah."

"Thanks."

Fallon smiled. *No problem, Riley—no problem at all.*

❧ ❧ ❧

"You look like shit," Carol observed.

"Don't hold back," Fallon replied.

"So?"

"What?"

"What do you mean, what? Who's the girl?"

"Riley?"

"I don't know. Is that her name? Riley? So…"

"Oh, my God, you think I took advantage of a woman stranded with her kid?"

"Did you?"

"No!"

Carol put her hands on her hips. Fallon's reaction was more defensive than she would have expected. She was, after all, teasing her friend. *Now, what is that about?* "So, what's her deal?"

"Riley?"

"No, Aunt Jemima. Of course, Riley."

"Oh." Fallon shrugged and started another pot of coffee. "She's moving into the Main's old place."

"Oh. Yeah, your mom mentioned that. Her husband died, right?"

Fallon nodded. For some reason, that thought made her stomach twist into knots. Riley was young, attractive, and from what Fallon had surmised kindhearted. She liked Riley. Being a single mom wasn't easy for anyone. Being a young, widowed, single mom, that had to have been hell. "Yeah."

"So, her car broke down?"

"Yep. Good thing I was here." That thought had passed through Fallon's mind numerous times throughout the night and morning. What would have happened to Riley and Owen if she hadn't found them? Riley had shivered well into the early morning. Sleeping in the car would have been dangerous, and without heat? Fallon shuddered.

"You okay?" Carol asked.

"Yeah. Just thinking that it could've been worse. Walking through the dark in a strange place with a toddler in a snow storm is bad enough. No place to sleep?"

"Well, you found her so…"

"Yeah." Fallon's phone buzzed. "Hey, you're up."

Carol moved to start another pot of coffee. A steady flow of drivers had been meandering into the pub over the last hour. She kept her eyes and ears trained to Fallon, interested in learning more about the newest addition to Whiskey Springs, and curious about the effect this Riley person seemed to have on Fallon. *What's up with you, Fallon?*

"I think Owen is done with sleep."

Fallon chuckled. She had a nephew and two goddaughters who had taught her that children made their schedule and thus yours. "Hungry?"

"A little. I think he is."

"I'll be up in a minute."

"Fallon, don't worry about us. Take your time."

"Carol's here. I'll be there in a minute."

"Okay. We'll be ready," Riley promised.

"Riley?" Carol guessed.

"Yeah. I guess Owen is her alarm clock."

"That's her kid?"

Fallon nodded. She grabbed her jacket and headed for the door when Pete blew in.

"Glad you're here," he said.

Fallon stopped. "Why do I not like the sound of that?"

"Well, you know how you asked me to go check on the Main place?"

"Yes?"

"Uh…"

"Pete?"

"Well, see the thing is…"

"Pete!"

"Um… There's kind of a tree on the roof." He braced himself.

Fallon threw her head back and groaned. "How bad?"

"Couldn't tell. No power though. Whole street is out."

"Shit." Fallon's hand swiped over her face with frustration.

"Hey, I'm sure that someone can let the lady stay for a few days or…"

"Or?"

Pete cringed. "I think the roof might need a little attention."

"Fuck."

"Hey, Dale has an extra room," he said. "You know Marge, she'll be…"

"I'm not worried about that," Fallon said. "Riley can stay with me. It's just a shitty way to start someplace new."

"Maybe your luck rubbed off on her," Pete said.

Fallon glared at him.

Pete held up his hands. "I'm uh… just gonna go tow that car now."

Fallon groaned. "What the hell else can go wrong?" Her phone rang again. She picked it up without looking. "Yeah?"

"Well, at least you're alive."

Shit. "I was supposed to text you."

"Are you okay?" Andi asked.

"Just tired. Long night."

"So, I heard."

"You heard? What did you hear?" Fallon asked.

"Saving lost souls?" Andi teased.

"Let me guess, Pete plowed your driveway." She looked at Pete.

"Good guess."

"I'm sorry I forgot to text you."

"Fallon, I'm just teasing you," Andi said.

Fallon sighed. She knew Andi was teasing. She also knew that Andi's concern for her welfare was genuine and well-placed. Last winter, a good friend of Andi's younger son was killed while he was shoveling his parents' walkway. A passing truck hit a patch of ice. The driver lost momentary control and hit Ted Donaldson. Storms were common place. They still carried danger. The incident had shaken the town. It had also left an impression on Andi. Dave Maguire had been outside clearing Andi's walkway about a quarter of a mile up the road from the Donaldson's. It could easily have been Dave and not Ted.

"I know you're teasing," Fallon said. "I also know you were worried."

"I know you can take care of yourself."

"Everything okay there?" Fallon asked.

"I'm fine," Andi promised. "I'll probably head down there later for a bite if you're planning on staying open."

"We'll be here. What about Jake?"

Andi sighed. "Stuck where he is until tomorrow."

"If you need me to come get you…"

"I'll manage," Andi said. "Are you sure you're all right?"

"Tired," Fallon repeated. "And, just got some unexpected news."

"Oh?"

"Nothing dire," Fallon promised. "I'll explain when I see you later."

"Okay."

"Just be careful driving."

"Now who's worrying?" Andi asked.

I do worry. "Seems fair."

"I suppose it does. See you in a bit."

Fallon shook her head. Normally, one of Jake Maguire's unexpected trip extensions would have thrilled her. Nothing about the last twenty-four hours felt normal. *I hope Riley doesn't freak out. I think I would.*

CHAPTER FOUR

Riley stared at Fallon blankly.

"Riley?"

"Are you telling me that I have no place to live?"

"No," Fallon said. "Just that there is a tree on the place you are planning to live."

"And, that's different how?"

"Around here, that's not all that unusual. Listen, I'll take a ride out there later and have a look. It's probably not that bad."

Riley's lips pursed.

Fallon chuckled. "Okay, I get it. This has been a rough start."

"That's an understatement."

"Nah. It's nothing we can't fix."

"Fallon, none of this is your problem."

Fallon's eyes narrowed. "I don't think it's a problem," she said. "It's just shit that happens. We'll figure it out."

"*We'll* figure it out? You don't need to figure anything out," Riley said. She sighed. "I should never have left San Diego."

Fallon looked at her feet.

"I'm sorry. You've been great. I just feel like this is some kind of sign."

"Maybe. That doesn't mean it's a sign that you're not supposed to be here."

Riley shook her head.

"Mommy!" Owen toddled over and lifted his arms.

Riley scooped him up. "I know, little man. You're hungry."

Fallon smiled. "Listen."

Riley looked at Fallon. She felt hopeless, and she felt like an imposition. None of her issues were Fallon's problem.

"Come down with me to the pub. We'll have something to eat and figure it out. It's a storm, Riley. Things happen—things like cars conking out and trees falling. It happens. It can all be fixed."

"You've already gone out of your way…"

"Not really," Fallon said. "You give me too much credit. I towed your car and let you crash for a night."

"And, made sure the car got to the garage, and gave us your bed, and came…"

"Okay," Fallon held up her hand and chuckled. "The thing is, anyone I know would have done the same thing."

Riley found that hard to believe.

"They would. At least, here they would. It's one of the things I like about living here. People are people, Riley. I'd be the first to tell you that sometimes people here drive me nuts. They do look out for each other, and that includes anyone who visits. Just don't give up on your decision to come here because of a few bumps."

"Speaking from experience?"

"Yeah, I am."

"Murphy's Law?"

"Something like that."

Riley sighed. "A tree, huh?"

"At least it was only one. Could've been a forest."

Riley couldn't help but smile. "I'll try to keep that in mind."

"Come on." Fallon opened the front door. "I make a mean pancake."

"Is that so?"

"Yeah, I have Aunt Jemima on my side."

Riley laughed. *What on earth have I gotten myself into?*

※ ※ ※

Owen spooned some scrambled eggs into his mouth and giggled at Fallon.

"He likes you," Riley observed.

"Probably because he knows he's smarter than me."

Riley rolled her eyes. She had noticed quite a few pictures of Fallon with children back at the house. She wondered if they were nieces and nephews or perhaps the children of a friend. Owen had gravitated to Fallon immediately. She let him stir the pancake batter and swirled him in the air before placing him in a booster seat. Riley had the sense that while *Murphy's Law* was a pub by night, it doubled as a family spot by day.

"Do you have a lot of kids come in here?" Riley asked.

"Depends on what you consider a lot," Fallon said. "It's a place people feel comfortable bringing their kids—mostly in the afternoon."

Owen grabbed a piece of pancake with his fingers and shoved it into his mouth. He reached out for Fallon and grinned.

Fallon laughed. "You're sticky, buddy."

"Fallon," Riley began cautiously. "What am I going to do?"

"You mean, where are you going to stay?"

"There is that."

Fallon concentrated on her plate. "You can stay at my place."

Riley set her fork down and stared at Fallon.

"I have two extra rooms," Fallon explained. "I didn't offer you the kids' room last night because it's been closed and I figured it'd be kind of cold in there. You were already…"

"I can't impose on you. There must be a hotel or…"

"There are a ton of places in Burlington," Fallon said. "And, there are a few B&B's in the area. Why would you waste money on that when you have someplace right here?"

Riley groaned.

"Seriously." Fallon finally met Riley's gaze. "I have a room for when my goddaughters visit. There's two beds in there. And, I have a guest room. Hell, you can have my room for all I care. I usually end up asleep in the chair anyway."

Riley looked at the ceiling. *What the hell am I supposed to do?* She didn't doubt that Fallon's offer was sincere. And, the truth was she wanted to accept. If she was going to try to make a go of it in Whiskey Springs, she would need to make friends. She'd like to count Fallon in that group. That was also part of the problem. Taking advantage of someone's kindness was not in Riley's nature. The last thing she wanted to do was wear out her welcome when she had just arrived. Bunking down at Fallon's in the middle of a blizzard was one thing; Fallon providing her with indefinite lodging was another. She was at war with herself.

"Oh, man." Fallon started laughing. "Your plate looks like the zombie apocalypse."

Riley's eyes moved to Owen's plate. He had squeezed ketchup onto his eggs and pancakes, and seemed to be delighting in eating a fistful of the rather repulsive mixture.

"Hope it tastes better than it looks," Fallon said.

Fallon seemed unfazed by everything. Her playfulness with Owen was obviously genuine just as her offer had been.

"He eats like you." Carol looked over Fallon's shoulder at Owen's plate. "You are never babysitting my kids," she told Fallon.

"Oh? Something you forgot to tell me? That butcher make a delivery I don't know about?" Fallon asked.

Riley chuckled at the banter.

"One of these days," Carol said.

"Yes?" Fallon replied. "One of these days Charlie's going to make a special delivery?"

"You're impossible," Carol said. She looked at Riley. "Watch her, Riley. Fallon seems like a good influence."

"What's that supposed to mean?" Fallon asked.

Carol's eyes traveled down to Fallon's plate. Riley and Fallon's eyes followed.

"What? I like ketchup," Fallon said.

Owen burst into a fit of laughter. "Mommy!" He called for Riley's attention. "Messy, Fawon!"

Riley's eyebrows raised in unison. Owen was articulate for two. She was surprised that he was spouting Fallon's name already. Then again, she'd repeated it at least a thousand times in the last—how many hours had it been? Riley shook off the thought. The expression on Fallon's face was priceless. Riley wasn't certain if Fallon was actually wounded by the teasing or if the pout was solely for Owen's benefit. It didn't matter. Either way, it was another moment that endeared Fallon to Riley. It felt like eons since Riley had made a friend so quickly. She'd never examined that reality until now. Strange—Riley had always made friends quickly—close friends. As a child, it hadn't been uncommon for Riley to meet someone in the morning and find herself having a sleepover that night. In college, Riley would invite people she met strolling across campus to her parties, often finding herself tangled in a mess of underclassmen on her dorm room floor. She and Robert had all kinds of friends they spent time with. After Owen was born, Riley joined some Mom's groups. Within days she was hosting get-togethers at the house and talking on the phone about new motherhood with the women in her groups. That had all changed when Robert died. Riley withdrew. She supposed that was normal. Grief took over. Mourning didn't come with a timetable. As she watched Fallon interact with Owen and Carol so effortlessly, Riley realized the culprit of the change in her life. It hadn't been *her* grief. It had been everyone's reaction to her grief. And, there it was again—the eggshells. *Maybe I should deem it eggshell theory.*

"Riley?"

"Huh?"

"You okay? Lost you there for a second," Fallon said.

"Sorry. I was just thinking about something. What did you say?"

"That I like ketchup."

Riley's smile failed to reach her eyes.

"Hey." Fallon reached over and covered Riley's hand. "I know it's been a little crazy. It really will be okay. We're not as crazy as we seem. Well, maybe we are but we're harmless."

"Fallon," Riley hesitated.

"What?"

"I would like to take you up on the offer."

Fallon grinned.

"But you have to let me help somehow."

"Help? Help with what?" Fallon asked.

"Whatever you need."

"It will probably only be a few days."

"Even so…"

"You're not going to let this go."

"No."

"Fawon!" Owen yelled.

Fallon jumped and looked back at Owen.

"Down, Fawon."

Riley looked on as Fallon wiped Owen's face and lifted him from his seat. His feet hit the floor and he raised his hands.

"Up, Fawon."

"Now, you want up?" Fallon picked Owen up and put him on her lap. He giggled.

"You're silly," Fallon tickled him. He laughed harder. She looked back at Riley. "I suck at laundry."

"What?"

"Me. I suck at laundry. I always mix up the baskets. You know, which one is dirty and which one is clean? I end up washing everything ten times."

"Uh-huh."

"So, for a couple of days you can help me with that."

"Laundry?" Riley asked.

Fallon shrugged. "I've got nothing else."

"Laundry it is then."

"How long do you think you'll have company?" Andi asked. She had met Riley briefly as Fallon was leaving to drive Riley and Owen back up the hill. Riley seemed friendly, albeit slightly frazzled. What struck Andi was how relaxed Fallon seemed. It didn't surprise her. Fallon would never admit it, but Andi knew she was lonely. It was part of the reason Fallon spent so much time everywhere and anywhere but home. Fallon had brightened measurably as she simultaneously made Andi's margarita and recapped her day with Riley Main, and the deal they had struck—lodging in exchange for laundry.

"Don't know," Fallon answered. "Depends on how familiar the tree got with the roof."

Fallon pulled into Andi's driveway. She had taken a ride with Riley out to the Main house to look at the situation. She hadn't been able to get close enough to tell how much damage the tree had done. A downed power line prevented her from making it all the way up the driveway. She'd assured Riley that they would get some answers in the next couple of days. When they got back to the pub, Pete was pulling in with Andi in his truck. It had worked out perfectly for Fallon. She had made the excuse that she wanted to check on her mother's house, so she could drop Andi home. She followed Andi to the door and let Andi close and lock it behind them.

"There is a bonus to this storm," Fallon said.

"Oh? You mean besides someone to do your laundry. I wondered why you were always wrinkled." Andi flung her coat over a chair, accepted Fallon's and tossed it aside.

Fallon pulled Andi into her arms. "Wrinkled? I'm not even forty yet."

Andi's eyes sparkled with affection and desire. She was thankful for this time with Fallon. Thankful for the playful twinkle she noted in Fallon's eyes. "Oh, less than a year, love."

"Nine months, Andi. That's a lifetime."

Andi took Fallon's face in her hands. She brought her lips to Fallon's. "You're shaking, Fallon. Are you cold?"

Cold? Andi could heat up an entire house with little more than a few words. Shaking? Fallon was positive the quivering in her body would seem like nothing shortly.

Andi's eyes danced. Her hands fell to Fallon's breasts. "Maybe you should go start a fire."

Fallon's eyes held Andi's steadily. "A fire?"

"Mm. I don't think I want to climb the stairs tonight."

Fallon swallowed hard. *One of these days she's going to kill me.*

Andi kissed Fallon softly. "Do you need to get home?" She teased.

"I don't have a curfew."

"Mm. You do have a guest."

"What guest?"

Andi licked her lips. "I'll get some wine."

"I don't need any wine."

"Start the fire, Fallon."

Fallon caught her breath as Andi walked into the kitchen.

Andi peered around the corner at Fallon as she readied the fireplace. She wanted Fallon, and she wanted to feel Fallon a certain way tonight. She had been tempted to push Fallon against the door and take her forcefully. Jake would be home tomorrow. Whether Fallon thought so, her life also just got a tad more complicated. Temporary guest? Perhaps that is what Riley Main would turn out to be. Andi was sure that Riley's stay at Fallon's home would be temporary. Something told her that Riley's presence might prove more permanent, and not just in Whiskey Springs. Fallon had talked about Riley and Owen more than Andi had heard her talk about anything other than the pub in years. Something about the young woman had intrigued Fallon. That much was evident. Andi suspected it was more than that. She would never leap to the conclusion that Riley represented the love Fallon claimed she didn't need in her life. Fallon could use a friend other than Carol who was also her employee, and other than Andi which carried its complications. She felt the winds of change at her back. Tonight, Andi wanted to take her time with Fallon. A fire, two glasses of wine, and Fallon—what else did she need? Nothing.

Fallon knelt in front of the fireplace. She felt Andi's hand on her shoulder before she saw the wine glass being offered to her. "So, a fire?" Fallon asked.

Andi sat on the plush rug next to Fallon. She sipped her wine and set it aside on the table behind them. "Are you going to taste it?"

Fallon set her glass next to Andi's. "Yes," she replied. Her lips tasted Andi's tentatively for a moment, her tongue sweeping across Andi's lower lip, tasting the sweetness of Chardonnay before requesting entrance. Sweet and warm, Andi's tongue caressed Fallon's, imploring her to explore. Fallon's heart sped up immediately. She pressed Andi backward onto the carpet and held her hands over her head. Her head dipped lower, her teeth nipping lightly at Andi's neck.

Andi's back arched, desperate for Fallon's touch. How had she ended up beneath Fallon? She had intended to place Fallon beneath her, to undress Fallon slowly and touch every inch of the body she constantly sought to memorize. She strained against Fallon's grip. Fallon pressed against her.

"No," Fallon whispered. "Not tonight, Andi. Tonight, I am going to touch every inch of you—every inch."

Andi moaned.

Fallon lifted Andi and relieved her of the soft, white sweater that had given only the vaguest hint of the treasures beneath. Fallon's eyes traveled to the swell of Andi's breasts. She wanted nothing between them. Methodically, Fallon removed every stitch of material that covered Andi's body. *Jesus, she is fucking hot.* She was. Andi exuded sexiness. She carried herself with confidence, not cockiness—assuredness that made her infinitely more attractive. Andi had edges, not just curves. Hard and soft, contrast and contradiction, gentle and demanding—it made Fallon's body sing.

"What were you thinking about last night?" Fallon asked.

Andi's eyes searched Fallon's. "You."

"Mm. What about me?" Fallon challenged. "You thought about this?" Fallon's tongue delicately circled one of Andi's nipples and then the other.

Andi moaned again.

"Mmm," Fallon hummed. "That?"

"Yes."

"Just that?" Fallon asked.

"No," Andi said.

"Show me," Fallon said.

"You need to be naked for me to show you."

Fallon smiled. "Is that what you want? Me naked."

"Yes."

"Right now?"

"Yes."

Fallon stood and slowly stripped for Andi, delighting in the way Andi's eyes followed her hands. "And?" Fallon asked.

Andi sat up and gripped Fallon's hips.

"Yes?" Fallon asked.

Andi pulled Fallon gently.

Fallon fell back to her knees. She shook her head. "No."

"No?"

"Right—no." Fallon pushed Andi back again and straddled her. "I've been thinking about you all day." Her tongue bathed Andi's neck and continued lower. "Thinking about you lying in bed last night touching yourself."

Andi's heart skipped wildly.

"Show me," Fallon directed.

Andi looked at Fallon to gauge the seriousness of the request. Fallon's eyes were fixed on hers. It was not a request; it was a direction. Andi watched as Fallon sat back on her heels, contemplating her. A deep breath and Andi let her hands fall to her breasts. Her fingertips danced over her nipples softly.

Fallon wondered if she would be able to hold her resolve. She desired Andi. She'd been fantasizing about this on and off all day, Andi touching herself, working herself into a frenzy while Fallon looked on. Just when Andi began to rise, Fallon would descend on her like a bird on unsuspecting prey and carry her away. That was Fallon's plan—if she could keep her mounting lust at bay long enough.

Andi recognized the haze in Fallon's eyes. She'd witnessed it many times. When Fallon did touch her, it wasn't going to be gentle; it was going to be urgent. Anticipation drove Andi on. She wanted to feel Fallon's power. She wanted to experience the power that coursed between them. Her fingers tugged at her nipples and her eyes closed. She heard Fallon's groan of frustration and smiled inwardly. She would not make this easy for Fallon. Torture could be a two-way street. As much as she wanted to feel Fallon's hands on her, Fallon's mouth over hers, Fallon's fingers inside her, what Andi desired most was to touch Fallon, taste Fallon, watch Fallon thrash beneath her, or perhaps above her until she shook uncontrollably. *And, I will.*

Fallon's tongue wet her drying lips. Her mouth had gone dry. She imagined it was because all the moisture in her body had suddenly pooled between her legs. Andi made her crave release. Andi made Fallon think about things that Fallon would never consider with someone else. She felt no sense of timidity in Andi's presence. She didn't need to prove her love or guard her fantasies. She could unleash unbridled passion, speak her deepest longings; not the hopes in her heart but the cravings that existed within lust. Nothing she said would drive Andi away. There was little if anything she could take or ask for that would cause Andi offense. Knowing that set something primal free from her soul.

Andi's hand dropped between her legs. She kept her eyes on Fallon. Fallon's eyes followed Andi's hand. Andi's back arched and her fingers began to slide up and down the length of her arousal. She moaned, more for Fallon's benefit than a need to release her mounting pleasure. And, her pleasure was mounting. "Mmmm." Her fingertip circled her clit over and over, just enough to heighten her desire. "What do you want Fallon?"

"No." Fallon held her ground. "You tell me what you want —what you imagine right now."

"I want to taste every inch of you," Andi answered honestly. "I want to be inside you. I want to hear you beg me to make you come."

Fallon bit the inside of her lip. That was not what she expected Andi to say, and God did she want Andi to do that. She had thought Andi would ask for Fallon to touch her. Andi was onto her game. Fallon leaned into her lover's ear. "Is that right?"

"Yes."

"That's what you want?"

"Mmm."

Fallon surprised Andi by dropping her breasts over Andi's mouth. Andi wasted no time. She craned to suck a nipple into her mouth. God, she loved Fallon's breasts. They were much larger than she had first imagined. Andi could touch and taste them for hours and not grow tired. She loved the way Fallon's breath would hitch and sputter when she played with them; the way Fallon's hips would lift and she would grip her lower lip with her teeth. Feeling Fallon sway above her made Andi dizzy. Fallon's movements were sensual and feminine. Instinctively, Andi's fingers began to circle her clit more forcefully. Touching Fallon aroused her past the point of sense.

Fallon grinned inwardly. "Tell me," she asked, stopping to moan when Andi's teeth raked over a sensitive nipple. "Tell me what you want right now."

Andi was gone. "Fuck me. Fallon…Please. I want you to fuck me."

That was it. Fallon tore herself away from Andi's eager tongue and descended her body languidly. She removed Andi's hand and tasted the length of Andi's need.

"Jesus!" Andi screamed.

"Not quite," Fallon replied playfully. She flipped Andi over and guided her to her knees.

Oh, God. Andi shouldn't have been surprised. She'd told Fallon what she wanted. Fallon was about to oblige.

Fallon's hands ran over Andi's ass tenderly. Her finger slid down the valley that separated two supple, quivering cheeks. "You are so wet," she breathed. She felt Andi's ass back into her, pleading for contact. Fallon entered Andi gently with two fingers.

"Oh… Yes… Fallon, please."

"Tell me," Fallon said. "Please what?"

"Please, fuck me. Fallon, please."

Fallon complied, thrusting into Andi deeply—in and out in long, soft but forceful strokes until Andi's ass moved to meet her in a well-timed rhythm. Fallon's eyes were riveted to the sight before her; the expanse of Andi's back as it stretched and contracted. Her creamy skin, and the way her hair brushed over her shoulders. The smoldering gaze in those grey eyes when Andi looked over her shoulder. Andi was hot. No, Andi was fucking hot. Everything about Andi turned Fallon on—everything. Not for the first time, Fallon found herself grateful that she had taken Andi as a lover. Sometimes, she missed making love. Sex with Andi never fell over that line. It hovered there. It never descended into the tender ripples of making love. Being with Andi was like walking through a tornado. It was swirling and violent. It sucked you up unexpectedly, turned you about until you lost all bearing, and then offered you one-second of complete silence before you crashed violently. It was nothing short of thrilling. No wonder people became storm chasers.

Andi's toes curled in time with Fallon's fingers. Fallon's thumb pressed against her clit, never making any move to explore. Each time Fallon thrust into her, Fallon's thumb would glide over that sensitive point, taking Andi higher. Her muscles gripped Fallon's fingers, desperate for release, desperate for Fallon. Her mind spun with images of Fallon hovering above her, tasting Fallon's breasts, playing until Fallon begged her for more. Right now, Andi would be happy to beg. She'd give Fallon anything she asked for—anything.

Fallon's center throbbed. God, she needed to feel Andi. She would be thinking about this night every day until they could repeat it. And, she was positive she would need to relieve the ache before then. It would never compare to this. "I want you to come," Fallon said.

Andi's head fell, her hips bucked, and she let herself go. *Anything you want, Fallon. Anything.*

Fallon's left hand gripped Andi's hip, holding her steady as Andi's orgasm threatened to send her to the floor. Fallon was not ready for that just yet. She moved tenderly in and out of Andi until Andi shuddered again softly. Then Fallon lowered her lover to the floor and kissed her.

"Get over me right now," Andi said.

Fallon's heart thundered in her ears. *Over her? Dear God, help me.* She did as Andi instructed and straddled Andi's face. Warmth spread over and through her. Her arousal mixed with the heat of Andi's mouth and the softness of Andi's tongue. Andi's tongue danced over Fallon in graceful strokes, teasing her until Fallon's hips began to gyrate side to side. Fallon struggled to stay upright.

Andi held Fallon in place, determined to keep her hovering until she had no choice but to fall. She could sense Fallon's frustration. She wished she could play Fallon's game now and ask Fallon what she wanted—tell Fallon when she wanted her to let go. She would never give up her prize, not even for that indulgence.

Fallon's knees were shaking. She needed to brace herself, but where? There was nothing to hold onto. *Jesus*. She didn't want to break the connection. Without warning, she was lifted and tossed about. "Fuck!" Fallon screamed and fell forward, her hands gripping the carpet. Andi was still holding onto her, refusing to stop. Fallon's orgasm rocked her from within. "Andi, Jesus!"

Not done yet. Andi sucked gently.

Light exploded behind Fallon's eyelids. She tried to peel herself away from Andi's grip. Andi continued to hold her in place. She sometimes forgot how strong her lover was. Andi's curves disguised her raw power. It was intoxicating. Fallon's body finally gave all it had. She collapsed beside her lover, spent but satiated.

Andi propped herself up to look at Fallon. "You make me crazy."

"Crazy?"

"Mm. Crazy with desire," Andi said.

Fallon kissed her. "I know what you mean."

"It's going to be a long week."

"I'm sure you will find something to occupy your time," Fallon said.

Andi smiled softly. She'd never regret taking Fallon as a lover—never. It did carry complications. She knew where Fallon's thoughts had traveled. Fallon was right. Andi would likely find herself in her husband's arms whispering endearments after a night of lovemaking. It would be gentle, even cautious. She would not find herself craving Fallon in those moments, just as she thought nothing of Jake when Fallon touched her. They were separate; both part of Andi's life, even part of her heart, but two entirely different worlds that could never come together. Fallon would likely be alone unless some chatty visitor at the pub invited her home. Assurances aside, Andi knew that reality caused Fallon some pain. It wasn't a broken heart. Perhaps it was the reminder that love seemed to elude Fallon.

Andi caressed Fallon's cheek tenderly. *You would be so easy to fall for.* "I *will* miss you."

Fallon smiled.

In my way, I always do. You would be, Fallon. You would be so easy to fall in love with, if only you would let someone close enough. "It's only a week," Andi said.

Yeah. It's only a week.

CHAPTER FIVE

Riley woke up and stretched. It took her a minute to remember where she was. The last few days seemed a blur. She inhaled a deep breath and snuggled beneath the warm blankets. Fallon had made every effort to make her feel at home. She'd barely seen Fallon in the last two days. It felt a bit strange living in Fallon's home without seeing her. She wondered if this was normal for her new friend. Fallon's home was beautiful. It was warm and comfortable. It felt like a home, not a house, yet Fallon seemed to avoid spending time here. It puzzled Riley. She hoped that Fallon wasn't avoiding her or worse, that her presence made Fallon uncomfortable in some way. She forced her eyes open and pulled herself from the warmth of the bed, surprised that Owen had not awakened her.

Riley slipped on a sweatshirt and meandered down the hallway toward the kitchen. The smell of coffee wafting through the air told her that Fallon was either home or had left recently. She stopped abruptly at the scene in the living room. Fallon was sitting on the floor in front of the fireplace sipping what Riley imagined was a cup of coffee. Owen was sitting on her lap chewing on a piece of toast. Riley was happier to see Fallon than she might have imagined and touched by the tender display. "Hey."

Fallon turned her head. "Hey, look who's up, buddy?" She spun them on the floor to face Riley.

Owen smiled at his mother and waved. "Toast, Mommy."

"Fallon made you toast?"

Owen nodded and chewed on his toast some more.

"You didn't have to do that," Riley said.

Fallon shrugged. "He found me. I needed coffee. He wanted toast. Worked out for us both."

Riley smiled.

"There's plenty of coffee in the pot," Fallon said.

"Can I get you anything?" Riley asked.

"Me? Nope. Me and Owen are good, I think. You good, buddy?"

"Good, Fawon!" Owen parroted Fallon's words.

Riley chuckled. Fallon seemed content to let Owen use her as a sofa. *Well, he's happy.* She strolled into the kitchen and poured herself some coffee. *I wonder what she's doing home?*

"So, what are you up to today?" Riley asked as she took a seat on the sofa.

"Funny you should ask."

"Uh-oh."

Fallon grimaced. She had gotten a call late the night before from her friend Jerry. Jerry had been out to look at Riley's roof. His news, while not dire, was not what Fallon knew Riley hoped for. By the time that Fallon had gotten back from the pub, Riley had been asleep. It was not something she wanted to discuss over the phone.

"Fallon?"

"Jerry went out to your place yesterday afternoon. You know, he works with most of the major insurance companies."

"Yes, I know. And, you trust him. I know. So?"

"Short version? You need a new roof."

Riley sighed.

"Good news? He can do it."

"Okay?"

"Bad news? It'll be a few weeks."

"A few weeks?" Riley gasped.

"Well, he has two other jobs going and from what he said, he thinks they need to take down some other branches that could cause you issues. Plus…"

"Plus?"

"Well, there's a couple of cracked windows he thinks should be replaced." Fallon rushed to finish her thought. "He's great, Riley. It's worth a little extra time. He'll get it all onto your insurance. Trust me."

Riley groaned. "Weeks? Fallon, I can't stay here for a few weeks."

"Why not?"

"Why not? I don't want to be in your way."

Fallon's face wrinkled with confusion. "In my way? You're not in my way."

Riley raised a brow in challenge. "My son thinks you are his personal sofa."

Fallon grinned. She enjoyed having Owen around. Fallon loved kids. "Well, at least I can feel useful."

"Fallon, I'm serious."

"So, am I. Oh, come on. Am I that bad?"

Riley detected a genuine hint of fear or maybe it was sadness in Fallon's voice. *What is that about?* "Bad? Fallon, you've hardly been here. I don't want to put you out of your home."

Home? That's a loose term. She had been busy. Her mother was away in Baltimore visiting her brother and his family. She had wanted to check on everything at Ida's house. This was a busy season for the pub as skiers passed through town, and she had been helping Charlie with a surprise for Carol. That's what had taken up most of her time. It had never occurred to her that her absence might appear as avoidance to her guest. It made sense. One thing that Fallon had already surmised about Riley Main; Riley's concern about being an imposition was genuine.

"You're not," Fallon said. "I've been kind of busy the last few days is all."

"I noticed."

"Yeah, but that has nothing to do with you and Owen. It has more to do with Carol."

"Why? Is Carol okay?"

"She's a pain in my ass." Fallon laughed. "I mean that in the nicest of ways."

Riley didn't need more time with Fallon to know that Fallon adored Carol.

Fallon set out to explain. "Charlie…"

"The butcher?"

"Right. Well, he and Carol have been seeing each other a while."

"So, I've heard."

"Yeah, well, seems Charlie would like that to become a permanent arrangement."

"You mean he wants to propose?"

"Yep. And, he can't, you know, take her away to some romantic inn or some exotic beach. Nope, not Charlie. He wants to throw her a big birthday party and ask in front of the whole damn town."

"Let me guess; he rooked you into helping plan it."

"No, he coerced me into planning it—all of it. Well, except the proposal part. He's on his own there. Proposing to Carol?" Fallon shuddered.

Riley laughed. "Anything I can help with?"

"Actually, there might be."

"Happy to help."

"I don't want you to worry about staying here. Seriously, I mean it. It's kind of nice to have someone here to talk to."

Riley smiled. *That wasn't easy for you to admit.* "Fallon, I want you to promise me that if us being here is too much, whether that's tomorrow or a week from now, I want you to promise me that you'll tell me."

"I will, but I won't need to."

"I'm serious."

"Why are you so worried about this?" Fallon wondered.

"Because." Riley looked at Owen sitting contentedly in Fallon's lap. "I feel like we're becoming friends."

"I thought we were friends."

"You know what I mean."

"I guess I do."

"I don't want anything to ruin that," Riley said. "This is all new for me. This place…"

"Feeling homesick?"

Was she? Riley hadn't pondered that at all. In fact, she hadn't given much thought to home since arriving in Whiskey Springs, at least, not in the sense that she missed it. It would be easier in San Diego, easier when roofs needed replacing and cars needed fixing. Would it be happier? Three days in Whiskey Springs and Riley had already been entertained by the likes of Daryl and Daryl, Carol, and had offers for babysitting from Pete's sister Marge. She'd even crossed paths with Andi Maguire, who Riley had noticed gazed rather affectionately at Fallon. Every reasonable bone in Riley's body said that she should feel like a foreigner in this place. For some unknown reason, she felt at ease. She was dreading the call she would need to make to Mary to update her older sister on her living arrangements. It would give Mary another reason to suggest that Riley head home. She could hear it now. *Just come home, Riley. I don't know what you were thinking.* Homesick? A person needed to have a home to feel homesick.

"No," Riley said honestly. "I just don't want to ruin a friendship before it even starts."

"Don't drink all my coffee and we'll be fine," Fallon said.

Riley did not seem amused.

"Okay," Fallon conceded defeat. "I'm trying to understand; I am. Real friendships are pretty hard to ruin, Riley. Trust me on that. What could you possibly do? Shrink one of my sweaters in that laundry you promised to help with?"

Riley sighed.

"I'm serious."

"So am I," Riley replied. "The point is that we don't know each other that well. Who knows what I might do to make you uncomfortable."

Fallon laughed.

"That's funny."

"Kind of."

Riley's gaze hardened.

"Oh, come on, Riley. Think about it. You offend you? You're staying in the token lesbian's house who owns the token bar in town? Don't you think it's me who should worry about offending you?"

Riley's expression softened. *That really worries you, doesn't it?* "Unless you plan on forcing yourself on me; I don't think you need to worry about that—at all. I don't care about that, Fallon. I have lots of lesbian friends."

Riley's revelation didn't surprise Fallon. Riley had taken Fallon's disclosure in stride. She'd neither raised the point nor avoided it. It had been on Fallon's mind. She could be an incurable flirt, even when she meant nothing by it. Riley was right about one thing; their friendship was new. The last thing that Fallon wanted was to offend Riley or make her uncomfortable in any way. She was relieved to clear the air. Maybe she had avoided Riley a bit. It was funny; she looked forward to seeing Riley and talking with her. Their conversations flowed easily and honestly.

"I get it," Fallon said. "I want you to stay," she said. And, she did. "It'll give us a chance to get to know each other. If you don't end up thinking I need professional help by the time your roof's done, I'll consider it a huge win."

"You mean like a maid?" Riley teased.

"Is my house that messy?"

"Only your laundry."

Fallon laughed. "So, you'll stay?"

"You promise. If I…"

"If you drink all my coffee, I'll throw you out in the snow."

Riley rolled her eyes. *You are impossible.* She moved to relieve Fallon of Owen.

"Fawon!" Owen protested.

"See? Owen knows a good thing when he finds it."

Riley smiled. *Yeah, I guess he does.*

⋇   ⋇   ⋇

Fallon smiled when Riley walked into the pub. Apparently, she had accepted Marge's offer to babysit Owen for a few hours. It had taken more than a little convincing. Fallon finally explained that it would be as much a favor to Marge as it could ever be a help to Riley. Marge had lost two babies in two years, one miscarriage and one still-born birth. Pete had told Fallon that he feared it might kill his sister. Marge's husband, Billy had left her six months after the second loss. The loss and Marge's depression proved too much for him to handle. Fallon couldn't begin to imagine the pain that Marge went through. Marge was a year younger than Fallon. Fallon had always liked the younger McCann. Pete was four years older than Fallon. She recalled him as boisterous bordering on obnoxious as a kid. Marge had always been sweet. She was the girl who never quite seemed to find where she fit in. When Billy Lloyd came to town it seemed that Marge's life had finally hit its stride. Now, at thirty-eight, Marge Lloyd's prospects for building a family had diminished greatly. It hurt Fallon to watch. Marge was a first-grade school teacher. She loved children. Life could be incredibly unfair. Fallon was positive hearing the story had changed Riley's mind. And, Fallon was grateful that Riley had changed her mind.

Ida Foster had arrived home early that morning. Tonight, Fallon had planned a welcome back party for her mother. At times, Ida drove Fallon crazy. She never sought to control Fallon, but she did like to offer "guidance" as she called it. Guidance—that was another word for Ida's candid observations about Fallon's life. It was never harsh and never judgmental. Ida did like to "guide." Fallon adored her mother. They'd grown closer after her father's death, and Fallon cherished their relationship. Whiskey Springs always felt slightly alien when Ida was away. At least, it did for Fallon; although, she would never admit that to her mother. She was anxious for Riley and Ida to meet.

Riley had been staying with Fallon for just over a week. Fallon was enjoying the company. It had been eight years since she'd come home to anyone. After Olivia left, Fallon had no interest in sharing her home with another person for any length of time. Her mother had gently suggested she consider a roommate. It would help with expenses, she had said. Fallon knew that was code for "maybe you won't be so lonely." Lonely? Maybe she was a little lonely. From Fallon's perspective, a roommate would have been a sad attempt to fill a void that no one could fill. No one was Olivia Nolan. There was only one Liv. She was the reason Fallon had built the house the way she had. She had been the soul of the house Fallon had built. Fallon had expected to share it with Olivia, with the family they had discussed creating together. That was the reason Fallon had a house at all. She didn't need one. What did she need a house for? She was barely home. There was no reason to be home. At least there hadn't been until recently.

"Looks like Riley caved," Carol commented.

Fallon's eyes stayed with Riley as Riley hung up her coat and headed toward the bar. "You made it."

"Miss the chance to meet the legend?" Riley said. "Never."

"How was Owen?"

"Oh, you know, fascinated by any human that isn't me," Riley said. "I'm beginning to wonder if I should worry."

Fallon chuckled. Owen was an agreeable little boy. He was appropriately curious and friendly. She enjoyed the toddler's attention, and as much as Fallon might try to deny it; she sought his affection. He delighted in her antics and playfulness.

But Owen had one mommy and he was completely in awe of her. Fallon marveled at the way his eyes would light up at the mere sound of Riley's voice when she entered a room. They shared a bond that went far beyond biology. It was the type of connection forged by loss. Even a baby could feel grief, could sense sadness and loneliness.

"Worry?" Fallon shook her head. "Riley, that kid has one word on repeat—Mommy."

"Funny, I thought it was Fawon."

Fallon grinned. "You could've brought him," she said.

"Oh, so he could follow you behind the bar and learn to mix drinks at two? I don't think so."

"I wouldn't teach him that."

Riley pursed her lips. "So, that wasn't you I heard discussing your idea for a new margarita with my son at the breakfast table?"

Carol chuckled.

"What are you laughing at?" Fallon looked at her friend. "I was thinking out loud is all." She turned back to Riley. "Speaking of margaritas; what can I get you?"

"I drove, remember?"

"So? Leave your car here or we can leave the truck here. We're going to the same place. I'm not drinking," Fallon reminded her. "When's the last time you had a drink?"

"I seem to recall being asked to try something called a Bimini Bimbo last night."

"Fallon, really? You brought one of those sorority girls home to Riley?" Carol teased.

"That would have taken me more time to finish," Riley said without missing a beat.

Fallon's jaw opened and closed soundlessly.

"Although, it was sweet." Riley looked at Fallon. "Something you wanted to tell us, Fallon?"

Carol's howl of laughter startled Pete and Dale as they walked in.

Fallon shook her head. *You certainly are full of surprises.* "Okay, Ms. Main, seeing as your experience with the bimbo was less than memorable, what can I offer you tonight?"

"Holy shit, Foster!" Pete said. "You hooked Riley up with a chic?"

Riley bit her lip to keep from laughing.

Fallon groaned and looked directly at her. "You're enjoying this, aren't you?"

Riley held her thumb and forefinger apart slightly in response.

"Remember what they say, Riley," Fallon said.

"What's that?" Riley asked.

"Turnabout is fair play," Fallon replied.

"Oh? I thought turnabout was foreplay?" Riley fired back.

Fallon nearly swallowed her tongue. *She is on a mission to embarrass me.*

"She's gotcha' there," Carol said. She leaned into Fallon's ear. "You might just have met your match."

Fallon grumbled. "What would you like?" Fallon asked.

"I thought you knew what everybody wanted before they ordered," Dale commented.

Fallon ignored him.

"Surprise me," Riley said.

Fallon was caught off guard by the sudden flutter in her stomach. *She's not flirting, Fallon. Get a grip. It's Riley, for God's sake.* She nodded.

"How's the car?" Pete asked Riley.

"Better than it was before," Riley said. "Thanks, Pete."

"Ah, no sweat. You know, Marge was all excited about getting to hang out with Owen tonight," he told Riley.

"I'm glad she was available," Riley said.

Riley had hemmed and hawed over the idea of having someone babysit. It seemed that everyone was eager to offer help in some way. Her first week in the town had been more eventful than she expected. It did turn out to have some benefits. Riley doubted that she would know half the people she did had her car not decided to keel over and die late at night. And, the storm? The massive branch that had poked a hole in the roof of her new abode provided her more time to get acquainted with her new neighbors. Most of all, it afforded her the opportunity to spend time getting to know Fallon. She hadn't expected to have a circle of friends so soon. At first, she'd been inclined to think the upheavals were a sign of impending doom. There was always a reason for everything that happened. Riley did believe that even if she sometimes found it difficult to accept. And, there was always a silver lining. Even in the middle of the darkest storm a person could always find a silver lining if she bothered to look. Her Nana had always told her that. When she had called Sylvia earlier that week to tell her about her arrival in Whiskey Springs, Robert's grandmother had given her a reminder.

"You arrived safely," Sylvia said.

"Safely yes, not uneventfully."

"Oh dear, dare I ask."

"Nothing horrible. My car decided to break down just when I got into town—as it started to snow."

"Oh, my."

"And, there might be a tree partially through my roof."

"Of the car?" Sylvia asked.

"No, of the house."

"Oh, no."

"Oh, yes." Riley laughed lightly. "Thank God for Fallon."

"Fallon? Fallon Foster?"

"Is there another Fallon here I should be on the lookout for?"

Sylvia chuckled. "Goodness, I hope not. I think one is all any town can take. So, you met Fallon?"

"Oh, you could say that. I'm staying with her."

"Took you in, huh?"

"Like a stray," Riley joked.

"She'll take good care of you, Riley. Fallon's a good girl—always was. Give you the shirt off her back, that one. And, then dance around naked just to drive her mother crazy."

Riley laughed. "I believe that."

"You should; it's the truth. Really? How are you doing?" Sylvia inquired.

"I'm okay. Can I be honest?"

"You can always be honest with me."

"I know." Riley sighed. "Part of me wonders if all this craziness is telling me something."

"You mean you wonder if it's telling you to go back to California," Sylvia surmised.

"Is it? God, Gram… Everything is upside down. I don't even have a place to live."

"I thought you were staying with Fallon."

"I am, but that's not what I mean. She doesn't even know me and…"

"She doesn't? You mean she didn't know you when she asked you to stay."

"Right. And, she's gone out of her way to make Owen and I feel at home."

"That's a bad thing?" Sylvia asked.

"No, but it's not her problem. Pete is fixing my car for next to nothing. And, Carol? She and Charlie brought over some of her nephew's old toys for Owen."

"Sounds to me like you found the silver lining."

"What?"

"Oh, Riley, I know how hard everything's been. You know I do. I know what it feels like to lose your place."

"I know you do, Gram."

"But there's always a silver lining, sweetheart. Live as long as I have, and you'll learn that. It takes some time to see it sometimes. It's always there. Sounds like you've made some friends already."

"Yeah, I guess so."

"You see? Silver linings. Try not to think the worst, Riley. As bad as anything gets, tomorrow comes. Sometimes, you find the purpose in things that happen without looking. Those are the easy times—when the answer seems to magically appear. Sometimes? Sometimes, you look so hard to find an answer that you don't realize it's been staring at you the whole time. Don't give up just yet."

"You sound like Fallon."

Sylvia laughed. "Well, she's got some chutzpah. She's a teddy bear underneath, a lot like her mother. You could do a lot worse for a friend."

"So I'm learning."

"It'll work out," Sylvia said. "You call me anytime. Let me know when Ida's back in town. I can't wait to hear all about it."

"I will, Gram. I love you."

"I love you too. Kiss the little boy for me."

"I will."

"Here you go," Fallon placed a drink in front of Riley.

"Do I want to know?"

Fallon shrugged.

Riley sipped from the glass cautiously. "A little tart."

Fallon grinned. "I thought I'd give you something that takes a little more time."

"What does a broad have to do to get a drink in this town?"

Fallon's eyes lit up.

Riley turned to see a tall, gray haired woman removing her coat. *Ida.* The legend herself had arrived. Riley's attention turned back to Fallon. Fallon's eyes sparkled as her mother approached. Riley found herself wondering if someday Owen might look at her the same way.

Fallon made her way around the bar and embraced her mother. "Hi, Mom."

"Hi, Mom?" Ida pulled back and grinned. She looked at Riley. "You must be Riley."

Riley smiled and extended her hand. "It's so nice to meet you, Mrs. Foster. I've heard so much about you."

"Ida, and don't believe one word of what my daughter or Sylvia's said."

"No don't," Fallon said. "Believe *every* word."

Riley snickered.

Ida inspected the glass in front of Riley, shook her head, and looked at Fallon. "She's been here a week and you're experimenting on her already?"

Fallon's cheeks colored and then swiftly paled.

Riley reached over and grabbed Fallon's hand. "No worse than what Owen has subjected her to at the dinner table."

Fallon laughed. Owen liked to experiment with his food. She imagined that he would enjoy dirt, mud, leaves, and anything he could get his hands into enticing. Owen's curiosity and playfulness amused Fallon endlessly. She envied the ability children had to find interest and excitement in the mundane. Nothing was ordinary in a child's world. Owen liked to paint with his food.

Ida waited for an explanation.

"I think Owen is practicing to become a painter or something," Fallon offered.

"A painter?" Riley asked as she sipped her drink.

"Well, yeah. He likes to make pictures with his food. I'll bet there's a future in that."

Riley's face contorted with disbelief.

"What?" Fallon asked. "Everything goes these days; imagine in another twenty years? He's a prodigy."

"Or he's two," Riley said.

Fallon shrugged. "Maybe he'll be a chef."

"Uh huh, or a gardener."

"I could use one of those."

Riley smiled. "You could use a lot of things."

Ida's gaze moved back and forth between her daughter and Riley as if she were watching a tennis match. Fallon had prattled on about Riley and Owen the last couple of times Ida had called. She'd heard plenty about the young woman from her best friend. Sylvia had shared Riley's struggles after losing Robert. Ida could scarcely imagine how difficult it must have been to lose a husband with a new baby. Fallon's father's death had sent Ida reeling. She'd tossed and turned for weeks without more than an hour's sleep. Her restlessness had prompted her to take on endless projects simply as a distraction. Without warning her grief had turned and she hadn't wanted to get out of bed at all for nearly a month. Her children were grown. Sylvia told Ida that she worried Riley might be reluctant to get out and meet people in Whiskey Springs. The display unraveling before her eyes convinced Ida that Riley had made at least one friend in town.

Finding friendship with Fallon hardly surprised Ida. Fallon was outgoing and charming. She had always connected with people easily—sometimes, too easily, Ida thought. Fallon was inherently trusting, or at least she had been. She had a habit of letting people in—all the way in without reservation. She saw the best in people. That's who Fallon had always been. She was easy to talk to, and genuinely interested in what people had to say. A fast friend, that was Fallon. Ida hadn't seen her daughter let anyone as close in many years. Disappointment and a broken heart hadn't hardened Fallon; it had left her cautious—exceedingly so. She wondered what it was about Riley Main that Fallon seemed to have shed her armor so quickly.

Ida cleared her throat. "Perhaps the prodigy can teach you how to get your mother a drink."

Fallon grinned. "He probably could except his mother won't let me teach him." She moved back to the bar to fix her mother something.

Riley rolled her eyes. "At least, let him learn to speak full sentences before you put him behind the bar."

"Why? Carol can't."

"What can't I do?" Carol asked. "Oh, hey, Ida. How was the trip?"

"Long."

"How are you?" Carol asked.

Ida looked at Fallon. "Thirsty."

Riley laughed. There it was again; the twinkle she'd noted in Fallon's eyes reflected in Ida's. She studied the pair. There was no way to deny the resemblance. Both women were tall; Riley placed Fallon at roughly 5'9". Ida was nearly eye to eye with her daughter, unlike Riley who had to look up to meet Fallon's eyes. Fallon had blue eyes which stood in contrast to her dark hair and olive skin. Riley marveled at the way Fallon's eyes changed in hue depending on what she wore. When Fallon wore light colors, her eyes reminded Riley of the ice that covers a pond in winter—a faint, clear blue. But when Fallon donned her navy blue jacket her eyes seemed to darken, resembling the evening sky. It added to Fallon's striking appearance. Riley envied that. Her eyes were the color of honey. Robert had always complimented her on her eyes. She'd always considered them common.

Riley thought the lively conversation over what Fallon was pouring into Ida's glass was the most entertainment she'd had in weeks. Ida's expressions mirrored Fallon's a great deal. She wondered if Ida's silver waves had once been Fallon's color, a dark brown that looked either black or faintly red depending on how the light hit it. Fallon's hair barely brushed her shoulders; Ida's flowed to the middle of her back. Hair color aside, anyone would guess their relation at first sight. Riley was so busy studying the two women, she'd lost track of their conversation. The sudden crestfallen expression on Fallon's face pulled her back to the present.

"You know, your brother asked when you plan on visiting," Ida said.

"It's busy season. You know that."

"It's a three-hour flight, Fallon. You could go for a few days."

"How's the drink?" Fallon asked Riley.

Ida shook her head.

"It's good," Riley replied. She tipped her head slightly at Fallon. *What is that about?*

"He could easily come up here, Mom."

"Mm. You know, Liv would like to see you too, so would the girls."

Fallon groaned. "Mom, don't."

"Don't what? You haven't gone down there to see them in over a year."

"Hey, sorry I'm late." Andi placed her jacket on a hook inside the door.

Fallon grinned, relieved to see Andi walk through the door. *Save me.* "Margarita?"

"Always," Andi replied.

"How was your trip?" Andi asked as she took a seat beside Ida.

"Long," Ida replied. "I barely recognized the kids. They've all grown so much."

"They were just here in August, Mom," Fallon said.

"That was months ago."

Fallon nodded. "Well, they'll be here in a few weeks for a whole week, so you'll get your fill."

Ida turned back to Andi. "How are the boys?"

"Oh, you know; busy as ever," Andi replied. "They're both doing well."

Fallon handed Andi her drink. Riley noted the way Fallon's fingers grazed Andi's hand tenderly.

"Thank you," Andi said.

"And, Jake?" Ida inquired.

"Home packing."

"Where's he off to now?" Ida wondered.

"Would you believe a conference in Cape Town?"

"South Africa?"

Andi nodded.

"Goodness, that's a long way to go."

"It is. He's there for two weeks and then off to Paris. He'll be gone an entire month."

Riley tried to conceal her interest by looking at the contents of her glass.

"Guess I didn't make it tart enough," Fallon commented.

Riley looked up.

Fallon sensed her discomfort. "You're almost dry," Fallon said. "Same thing?"

Riley smiled. "What does Jake do?" she asked Andi.

"He was a thoracic surgeon," Andi replied.

"Was?"

"Yeah. He works for a company that designs new surgical tools."

"Must be interesting," Riley said.

"I'm sure it is," Andi chuckled. "I confess; I don't understand half of what he tells me. He loves it, though."

"What about you?" Andi asked.

"Me?" Riley replied.

"Fallon mentioned something about you being a writer."

Riley blushed. "One day I hope to add that to my resume. I'm an editor—mostly mystery and romance."

"Sounds like the story of Fallon's life," Carol poked.

Ida laughed. "She has a point."

"She always has a point," Fallon said. "I just wish she'd aim it at someone else once in a while."

"Oh, relax." Carol patted Fallon's shoulder. "Everyone likes a little intrigue with their romance."

Andi smirked and looked into her glass.

"What did I do to deserve this?" Fallon asked.

"Hey, you're the one who wanted to play with drunk people all day," Ida said.

"Are you drunk?" Fallon asked.

"Will be if you ever get around to refilling this glass."
Riley laughed. *What a cast of characters.*

⚜ ⚜ ⚜

Fallon tossed her keys on the kitchen counter and went in
search of Riley. Andi had offered to drop Riley off before
heading home. Fallon was torn between wanting to thank Andi
and throttling her for leaving her to fend off Ida's "guidance"
for another hour. Ida had thrown back a few more drinks before Fallon put her in the car and took her home. Fallon was
exhausted. Her mother had the best of intentions. Fallon
wished that Ida could let certain things go; things like trying to
persuade her to visit Olivia and the girls in Washington DC.

"Hey," Riley looked up from the book in her lap.

"I wasn't sure you'd still be up."

Riley closed the book and set it aside. "You look tired."

"Probably because I am." Fallon flopped into her favorite
chair.

"Are you okay?"

"Me? Sure," Fallon said.

Riley's skepticism was obvious.

"I love my mom; I do."

"But?"

"Sometimes she doesn't know when to say when."

"You mean with alcohol?"

"No, I mean with her mouth. Alcohol doesn't help with
that," Fallon explained.

Riley nodded. "I should probably let you relax."

"I'm not kicking you out of the room."

"I know, but I can read anywhere. You seem to like to sleep
in that chair," Riley said.

True. I do love this chair. Fallon rarely slept in her bed. The
truth was it felt empty. A king-size bed was not meant for one
person. Fallon felt like she might be swallowed whole in the

middle of the night. Maybe it was loneliness that she feared might consume her if she spent too much time in that great big bed. There was no one to reach for, no tether. Fallon's thoughts whirled or perhaps it was her emotions.

"Fallon?"

"Sorry. I don't think I'll be sleeping any time soon."

"How about we trade?"

"You want the chair?"

Riley laughed. "No. I was going to suggest that I go make us a drink and you relax here."

"Seriously?"

"It will probably entail me popping open the bottle of wine I bought earlier and pouring it into two glasses."

Fallon grinned. "Easy is always best."

"So? Wine?"

"Sure."

Riley set off for the kitchen. *What is going on with her?* It would've been impossible to deny the connection between Fallon and Andi. Riley had surmised earlier that week that the two were close friends. She suspected their friendship extended into deeper emotions. And, Ida? Everything she'd heard about Ida Foster failed to capture the woman she had met. What was larger than life? Riley had been pondering how to describe Fallon's mother all evening. Larger than life seemed an inadequate characterization, and Ida was a character. Ida had gently teased Fallon, Carol, and Andi for over an hour. When Pete and Dale had wandered up to the bar she had instructed Fallon to turn the jukebox on and coaxed them into singing *Sweet Caroline* with her. But Riley had also noticed that some of the banter did not sit well with Fallon.

"Here you go." Riley handed Fallon a glass.

"Thanks. Listen, I'm sorry if things got a little weird earlier."

"Weird?"

"You know, with my mom. Her brain and her mouth don't always consult each other."

Riley chuckled. "I noticed that."

"Why she constantly presses me to visit Dean and Liv is beyond me."

"Liv?"

Fallon nodded. "Olivia. She's my ex."

"Ah. She's still close to your mom, I take it?"

"She's close to all of us." Fallon pointed to the photo of her goddaughters. "Emily and Summer are Liv's kids."

Riley was surprised.

"Yeah, I know. Kind of strange, isn't it?"

"Not unless it's strange to you."

"Not really," Fallon said. "Liv was one of Dean's best friends. That's how we met. She's three years older than me—three years younger than him."

"How long were you together?"

"Almost four years. Lived together for two. She left right after the house was finished."

"Ugh."

"Yeah, no kidding."

"Fallon, you don't have to tell me any of this."

Fallon sighed heavily. She wanted to tell Riley. It had been a long time since she had traversed this topic with anyone. Olivia would always be part of Fallon's life. Most of the time she was grateful for that. Occasionally, it caused her stress. Forgiveness had been easier to give than most people might have imagined. Forgetting the life they had shared was impossible. Worse, Fallon found herself confronting the life she and Olivia had planned over and over, except it was someone else's life. Olivia's decision to leave Whiskey Springs broke Fallon's heart. She accepted it. Part of her would always love Olivia Nolan. It seemed that every time Fallon thought she'd crossed the bridge that would keep her from drowning in the past, something or someone found a way to throw her back in the river that was Olivia, or more accurately the life she had planned with Olivia.

"She decided to take a job at The State Department in DC," Fallon explained.

"You didn't want to go?"

"No." Fallon sipped her wine. "It was out of the blue. At least, it was out of the blue for me. One day we were building this house, talking about having a family and the next she was telling me she wanted to move."

"I'm sorry, Fallon."

"Yeah, I was too. She had a great offer to teach here—political science," Fallon explained. "I thought… Well, it doesn't matter what I thought."

"But you stayed friends."

"Yeah. We did. It took some time. She insisted I could work anywhere. I built this place for us. And, the pub? I didn't want *a* pub. I created *Murphy's Law*. I wasn't going to leave my life here, not even for her. Once she left… Well, we took some time. It took six months for us to see each other again. Two months later she was with Barb." Fallon took a sip from her wine to steady herself. "Our friendship almost derailed when she and Barb decided to have Emily."

"Barb?"

"Yeah, Liv's wife. She's a professor at Georgetown."

"What happened?"

Fallon took a deep breath. "We'd talked a lot about having kids. It was… It was something we both wanted. That's why this house is so big," Fallon explained. "It seemed logical." She took a deep breath. "Well, we approached Dean—you know, to be our donor?"

Riley's heart lodged in her chest. "Fallon, are you telling me that your goddaughters are your brother's kids?"

"Biologically—yes."

"Whoa."

"Mm. Like I said, they were friends before I met Liv. I guess she didn't see any need to change that plan after I was out of the picture. It took me a little time to process that."

"I can imagine."

Fallon smiled. "Don't get me wrong, it was between them. I get that. She's with Barb. It was their decision. It was Dean's. It didn't have anything to do with me. I just couldn't help but feel betrayed, I guess. It hurt." *There, I said it. It did.*

I would imagine so. "And, now?"

"Now? The kids are great. Barb is great. I love it when they visit. They come up twice a year. Emily's quite the little skier." Fallon laughed. "She should probably be named Winter. Summer? Well, she got her name for a reason. She's only four. Who knows? Maybe in a couple of years she'll grow to love it like Em."

"Sounds like you're close."

"As close as you can be when five-hundred miles is between you."

"And, Dean?"

"Dean?" Fallon laughed. "He's Dean. You'll like him."

"Oh? You think so?"

"Yeah, you'll like Liv too. Everyone does," Fallon said. "He and his wife, Beth won't be coming up with my nephew, Evan this trip. Liv is bringing them all up here during their February vacation."

"When is that?"

"Three weeks," Fallon said. "Liv will stay Friday night until Sunday morning. Then she flies home until Friday night. She'll drive the kids back on the following Sunday."

"Three kids all to yourself?"

Fallon shrugged.

"No wonder you're a pro with Owen. What about the pub?"

"I take three weeks off every year. Two for when the kids visit and one just for me."

Riley wondered how that worked. Fallon had a difficult time staying away from the pub for one day; an entire week? She giggled.

"What?" Fallon asked.

"Oh, nothing."

"Oh, come on, I just told you all about my ex."

"I'm just wondering how you plan to stay away from the pub for a week."

Fallon frowned.

I knew it. "Have you ever?"

"Have I ever what?"

"Made it one whole week without going into *Murphy's Law?*"

Fallon took a deep breath and huffed.

"I knew it!"

"I can do it," Fallon said. "I just choose not to do it."

"Right."

"I can."

"Really?"

"Yes, really."

"Care to make a wager?" Riley asked.

"You want to bet me that I can't stay away from work?"

"Yep. I like my odds."

"Okay. What are we betting? I want to know if this is worth my while," Fallon said.

Riley thought for a minute. "I will do your laundry for a month. Consider me your laundry service."

"You'll come here and do my laundry?"

"Yes. If you stay out of the pub for the entire week the kids are here."

"Uh huh, and what do you get if I fail?"

Riley grinned. "You teach me to tend bar."

"You want to learn how to tend the bar?"

Riley shrugged. "Hey, you never know when I might need something to fall back on."

JA ARMSTRONG

"You're serious? That's your bet?"

"Totally serious. Why? You think it's unfair?" Riley asked.

Fallon shook her head. It was more than fair from Fallon's point of view. She'd be happy to teach Riley to tend bar without any bet. "I don't think it's an even exchange."

"What do you mean?" Riley wondered.

"You've seen my laundry."

Riley sniggered. *True. You do manage to make a mess.* She had begun to wonder if Fallon's job was pouring drinks or wearing them. Fallon wasn't joking about confusing her laundry. It made no sense to Riley. Fallon's home was clean and organized. It was lived-in, not antiseptic, but it was hardly messy. Fallon was not the type of person who needed all the spoons facing the same direction or all the towels to be folded a certain way. She did take pride in her home as she did in herself. Riley had also learned that Fallon was adept at all kinds of tasks and trades. She might not have been an expert, but Fallon possessed a cursory knowledge of everything from car engines to potty-training. How was it that someone like Fallon failed to comprehend a simple task like laundry? *You are a bit of a mystery.*

"I think we need to sweeten the deal," Fallon surmised.

"For whom?"

"For you. I mean, either way I win; right? I get help at the bar or I get my laundry done. You don't gamble much, do you?"

Oh, you might be surprised. "What do you suggest, Ms. Foster?"

"I'll think of something."

"You want me to bet without knowing…"

"What you win?" Fallon interjected. "Don't you trust me?"

Riley smiled. Fallon was issuing her a challenge. "Okay. It's a bet."

"I wouldn't start learning your tequilas just yet."

"We'll see," Riley said. "We'll see."

CHAPTER SIX

Three Weeks Later

Fallon stretched and pulled Andi close. "I can't believe we have another week to be together and the kids will be here."

Andi held Fallon's arm around her. "We'll see each other at some point."

"It's not the same."

"No, it isn't," Andi agreed. She turned to look at Fallon and smiled. "I know that you're excited for the kids to get here."

"Mmm."

Andi sighed. "What is it? Is it Liv?"

"No. I don't know," Fallon admitted. "It's just strange having her there sometimes."

"I can imagine that's true."

"Sometimes, Andi…"

"What?"

"It still hurts. Seeing her in that house. The kids being there with her. It's been eight years. It still hurts."

Andi leaned in and kissed Fallon softly. "I know it does."

"I don't think I'll ever get it."

"Why she left?" Andi guessed.

"That. Why she wanted to stay friends."

"Why do you?"

Fallon's head fell back onto her pillow. "I didn't at first."

"Then why?"

"I don't know how to answer that. It's not like I had much choice."

"Because of your mother?" Andi asked.

"And Dean."

Andi placed her head onto Fallon's breast. "What about now?"

"I'm not in love with her, if that's what you're thinking."

I know that. "I'm not thinking anything. That's why I asked."

"I'm sorry. I wish Riley was still there."

Riley had moved into her home the previous week. Fallon had helped. Pete and Dale had pitched in. Even Andi had stopped by with dinner. Fallon had talked to Riley every day. She hadn't seen Riley for more than a few minutes in passing in almost a week. It felt strange. She'd found herself spending more hours at the pub than usual. Home felt empty—again.

Ah ha. "At your house?"

"Yeah."

Missing Riley a little, huh? "Why don't you ask Riley over on Saturday when Liv is there?"

"And what would I give as the reason?"

"How about the truth?"

"Which is?"

"You miss her and you want to see her," Andi said.

Fallon groaned.

"Why is that so hard for you?" Andi asked. "She's your friend, isn't she?"

"Yeah, she is. She just got settled. I doubt she wants to come hang out with my ex and her kids."

"I think you should call her. Owen would probably love to be around some kids."

"Maybe."

Andi moved to straddle Fallon. *You are so beautiful, Fallon.* Her lips brushed across Fallon's. *I wish you would give yourself a chance, love.* "Kiss me," she said.

⁂ ⁂ ⁂

"Hey, Riley!"

Riley turned to the sound of a familiar voice. "Hi, Jerry."

"How's the house?"

"Pretty good, actually. We're settling in. Thanks for every-thing. Your guys did a great job on the roof."

"Good. That's good." Jerry shoved his hands into his pockets. "So? How are you liking Whiskey Springs?"

"It's been an interesting few weeks."

"Yeah. Fallon mentioned your car shit the bed too."

Riley chuckled.

Jerry looked down at Owen. "Sorry."

"It's okay. It was good to see you, Jerry."

"Yeah, you too."

Riley smiled, waved and headed for her car.

"Mommy, Fawon?"

Owen had been asking to see Fallon for days. "You're miss-ing your playmate, aren't you?" *I kind of miss her too.* "Do you want to go see if Fallon's at work?"

"Fawon!"

Riley laughed. "Guess that answers that question. Okay, little man, let's go see if we can find Fallon."

⁂ ⁂ ⁂

"When does Liv get in?" Carol asked.

"Tomorrow night. Sometime after dinner."

"Did you clean the house?"

Fallon glared at Carol. "What makes you think it was dirty?"

"You don't have live in help anymore."

"Very funny. I'll have you know…"

Carol's eyes tracked to the door. "Speaking of."

"Speaking of what? My dirty house?"

"Can't blame Owen this time," Riley said.

Fallon turned. "Riley?"

"Last I checked."

"Fawon!" Owen ran for Fallon.

Fallon swept him off his feet. "Hey, buddy. I missed you."

Owen's wide grin nearly stopped Riley's heart. He adored Fallon. Fallon hadn't just become Riley's friend, she'd captured Owen's imagination.

"Juice, Fawon."

"I don't know, buddy. We have to ask Mommy."

"Mommy, juice?"

"Yes, you can have juice." Riley reached in her bag and handed Fallon a sippy-cup.

"I'm glad you stopped in," Fallon said.

"I wasn't sure you'd be here," Riley replied lightly.

"Ha-ha. I'm going to win that bet," Fallon said.

"What bet?" Carol asked.

"Riley bet me that I can't stay away from the pub for the whole week."

Carol smiled. "Good bet, Riley. What did you ask for?"

"Hey!" Fallon shot. "I'm right here."

"So?" Carol rolled her eyes. "In the eight years I have been here, the longest you have ever stayed away was four days and that was when Ida was in the hospital. So, what do you get if you manage to leave us alone for an entire week?"

Fallon handed Owen his juice.

"Well?" Carol urged.

"Riley will do my laundry for a month."

Carol shuddered. "You are a brave woman, Riley. Good thing you're going to win."

"She's not going to win."

Owen giggled. "Fawon, sing!"

"Sing?" Carol asked.

Riley pursed her lips. She'd caught Fallon singing with and to Owen a few times.

"Fallon, are you going to sing for us?" Carol teased.

"Fallon's singing?" Dale asked as he approached the bar. "Oh, hey, Riley."

"Hi, Dale."

"What are you singing?" Dale asked.

"I'm not singing," Fallon said.

"Sing, Fawon!" Owen said and then laughed.

Fallon sighed. *I'm not getting out of this.* "How about we go play a song on the jukebox?"

Owen smiled and reached out for her.

Riley whispered in her ear. "Dodged a bullet, huh?"

"Owen, my boy, I thought we were friends," Fallon said. He laughed harder. "Is everything I say funny?"

"Funny, Fawon."

"Glad you think so."

Riley shook her head affectionately.

"Did you really bet her?" Carol asked.

"Yep."

"What do you get if she loses?" Pete asked.

"Well, other than the fact that she has to teach me how to tend the bar, I don't know."

"What? She managed to get you to agree to that?" Carol asked.

"That was my idea."

"Why?" Carol asked.

"Call it research," Riley said. Her brief time in Whiskey Springs had prompted an idea for a story; one about a small-town tavern and the slightly mischievous, tender-hearted woman behind the bar.

Riley's ears perked to the sound of *Brown Eyed Girl*. Fallon was dancing with a giggling Owen and singing to him. *Pushover*.

Andi strolled into the bar. Her eyes immediately fell on Fallon in the distance. Fallon seemed oblivious to the world, completely engaged in Owen's attention. She meandered to the bar and took a seat beside Riley. Riley's gaze was fixed to the scene a few feet away. Andi watched Riley's expression thoughtfully. And, there it was—affection. She felt her heart lurch slightly. *Oh, Fallon, do you even see it?*

"Fallon found her dancing feet, I see," Andi commented.

"I don't think Owen gave her much choice."

Andi smiled. *Don't kid yourself, Riley; she loves every second of it.*

"Hey, Andi," Carol greeted her friend. "Margarita?"

"How about a martini instead?" Andi suggested.

"A martini?" Carol questioned.

"Dirty, if you would."

"Wow." Carol was surprised. Andi was predictable.

"Sometimes, you have to make a change before it's made for you," Andi offered.

Riley turned her attention to Andi. She liked Andi. She was certain she detected a note of sorrow in Andi's voice. "You okay?" Riley asked.

"I'm good." Andi squeezed Riley's hand. "Don't look now. Here comes Fred Astaire."

"Hey," Fallon said. "When did you get here?"

"I got here in time to see your fancy footwork," Andi teased.

"I have some moves."

Andi's eyes sparkled. *Yes, you do.* "Quite the handsome partner you have," Andi said.

"I know. He's the only man I'll let take me on the dance floor," Fallon said.

Owen laughed.

Fallon shrugged.

"And, the only one who will laugh at all your jokes," Andi said.

"Mm. I don't have to say anything for you to laugh, do I?" Fallon tickled Owen. He laughed some more. "Am I funny looking or something?" She made a face at him.

Riley rolled her eyes. *You are such a goofball.* "So? When does your company arrive?"

Fallon handed Owen back to Riley. "Tomorrow night."

"Excited?" Riley wondered.

"I'm not sure that's the word I'd use," Fallon said. Andi silently implored Fallon with her eyes. Fallon sighed. "About that," she said to Riley.

"What?" Riley wondered.

"I was kind of wondering if you were free on Saturday."

"Me?" Riley asked.

"And Owen."

"Let's see. I have a hot date with grocery shopping. Exciting, I know. I like to live on the edge."

"Well, would you maybe like to come over and have dinner at my place?"

Riley was puzzled.

"Feel free to say no," Fallon said. "I was going to cook out on the grill. For some reason, the kids seem to think grilling in the freezing cold is fun. Come to think of it; it's probably watching me grill in the freezing cold."

"What can I bring?" Riley asked.

"Bring?"

"Yeah, you know, *bring*—dessert? Wine? Juice boxes? What can I *bring*?"

"Oh. Nothing," Fallon said. "We'll probably fire up the grill around four. Can you come over around two?"

"Sure."

Fallon smiled. "Great."

Carol handed Andi her drink.

"What is that?" Fallon asked.

"What does it look like?" Andi replied.

"Since when do you drink martinis?"

"Sometimes, it's good to try something new," Andi said.

Fallon wrinkled her nose. "If you say so."

Andi smiled. *Oh, Fallon.*

Riley pondered the interaction. Fallon had never admitted to her affair with Andi. It was obvious to Riley. There was a unique way lovers communicated. Andi and Fallon shared that. She wondered what had brought them together. It seemed clear that Andi loved her husband, but her feelings for Fallon were also palpable. And, Fallon? Well, Fallon clearly cared for Andi Maguire. Riley didn't get the impression that they were in love. *Interesting.* It was curious to her. She'd only been with Robert for seven years before she had lost him. In many ways, she thought they were still in the honeymoon phase of their relationship. She was no stranger to extra-marital affairs. Her father and mother had both been unfaithful in their marriage. When Riley turned eighteen, they divorced. It had seemed odd to most of Riley's friends; there was no animosity in the separation. Brenda and Doug Fitzgerald had parted friends. Riley's mother purchased a condo in Seattle and her father relocated to his hometown in Colorado. Doug remarried the following year. Riley loved both her parents. She had been surprised when her father chose to delve into the topic of their marriage before his wedding.

"I don't want you to think that we didn't love each other," he said.

"I don't think that, Dad."

"I still love your mother."

"You know that doesn't make sense," Riley replied.

"No? Well, pumpkin, someday you might understand. We had different interests—other than you and your sister."

Riley nodded. That seemed obvious.

"I don't mean the affairs, Riley," he clarified.

"Dad, this is none of my business."

"Maybe not," he admitted. "I hope when you find that someone, I hope that it's forever, Riley. If it isn't, I hope you'll remember that it's okay to let go."

"Why didn't you?"

Doug shook his head.

"You and Mom. If you wanted to be with other people, why didn't you break up?"

"I loved her. We loved you and Mary."

"I don't get it. You stayed together for us?"

"That was part of it. We loved being with you—all of us being together."

Riley took a deep breath. "How did it start?" There, she asked. She wanted to know.

"You mean, who cheated first?"

Riley nodded.

"I did."

She nodded again.

Doug sighed heavily. "For years, she stayed faithful. Then she met Gil. I couldn't blame her. How could I? It hurt. It did, even if I had no right to feel that way. I realized how she must've felt all those years. When I met Lisa, your mother—Well, it was different. She sat me down and told me it was time for us both to move on."

"I don't know what to say."

"You don't need to say a thing. Just remember that life isn't all neat and tidy the way we like to think. It's a God dammed mess half the time. And, that's okay. That's all I'm trying to say. Hopefully, one day you'll find that person that eclipses all the rest."

"Have you?" Riley asked.

Doug smiled. "I hope so, Riley. I hope so."

"Jake comes home soon, right?" Riley asked Andi.

"Next Saturday," Andi replied. "He'll be home for three weeks before he's off again."

"That must be hard."

"Sometimes, it is." Andi sipped her martini. *Something tells me it might get harder soon.* She smiled at Riley.

Riley still held a degree of innocence. Andi envied that. She remembered that too. There were different kinds of loss. Infidelity was not the same as death. Both stripped a person of a degree of innocence, but in different ways. At forty-six, Andi had been with Jake Maguire for more than half her life. She'd raised two sons to adulthood. She'd mourned the loss of her mother and more people she loved than she cared to count. She tried to recall being thirty. A lot of living happened in sixteen years—a lot of living and a lot of learning. She was positive that Riley had caught onto her relationship with Fallon. Riley might have been young, she was not clueless. Riley had spent long hours with Fallon, and shared more than a few hours getting to know Andi as well. Andi watched as Fallon walked into the kitchen.

Owen wiggled in Riley's grasp. "Fawon!"

Fallon turned around. "Well, come on. You can help me do some dishes."

Riley laughed. *Great, an excuse for you two to play in the water.*

Andi watched as Fallon took Owen's hand and led him away. She took a deep breath. "You're wondering about me and Fallon."

"What? No. Andi, I'm not..."

"It's okay," Andi said. "I don't think it's the best kept secret in town." She chuckled. "Fallon likes to think so."

"Andi..."

"Riley, relax." She glanced to ensure Fallon was still in the other room. "I'm not in love with her," she said. "She's not in love with me either."

Riley suddenly felt uncomfortable. She hadn't intended to pry into Andi's life or Fallon's for that matter. It seemed that Andi needed to say something.

"I love her, though." Andi sighed. *I do.* "It's safe. Sounds crazy, I know. It's safe for both of us. Different reasons, I guess. It's safe." *Although, it doesn't feel all that safe right now.* "Sad, huh?"

"No," Riley said honestly. "Just human."

Andi pushed back a few tears. "Safe," she repeated. "Not always easy."

Riley nodded. Her thoughts traveled to her parents. Brenda Fitzgerald remained single. She'd continued to see Gil for two years after her divorce from Riley's father. She dated, but Riley had not seen her mother involved with anyone for more than seven years. She asked her mother once if she was lonely.

"I spent years feeling lonely when I was with someone," Brenda told her daughter.

"You mean with Dad."

"Well, he was off on his trips. First it was business, then it was golfing. You know your father. He's always been a bit of a nomad." She chuckled. "Then I met Gil."

"What happened with you two?"

"Me and Gil? Are you asking why we stopped seeing each other?"
Riley nodded.

"I love Gil—in my way. Gil and I were always friends."
Riley laughed. "Friends with benefits?"

"Yes," Brenda replied honestly. "That's a good way to describe it. I loved him. Still do. I miss him sometimes."

"You still talk to him; don't you?"

"Sure. We have a drink every so often too. That's the extent of it."
"Don't you want to find someone?"

"I don't know. I'm not looking for it. Would I like to be in love? Who wouldn't?" Brenda laughed. "That's the thing; I just don't feel the need for those fringe benefits anymore."

Riley was shocked. Her mother was only in her fifties. "You don't want to have sex anymore?"

Brenda laughed raucously. "You are too much sometimes. What do you think? You shrivel up at fifty?"

"No. You're the one who said you didn't need fringe benefits."

"I suppose I did. How do I explain this? I've been in love. I've had a lover. I guess, I would like them in tandem. If I'm going to invest myself in someone; I want more than what I had with Gil or your father. I want to be enough for that person."

"Mom…"

"And, I want that person to be enough for me. Until then, I have to be enough for me."

"She cares about you," Riley told Andi.

Andi grinned. *She cares about you too—more than she's ready to admit.* "I know she does. I care about her."

"I can see that."

"Mm. She cares about you too, Riley."

Riley smiled. "Fallon's... Well, she's become a good friend. Honestly, I don't know what I would do without her."

Andi nodded. *I know the feeling.*

Fallon chose that moment to walk out of the kitchen.

"Fawon!" Owen laughed. "Down!"

Fallon set Owen on his feet and handed him a dollar. "You know where the stool is?"

He nodded.

"Good. Go put this in the jukebox like I showed you. Then Mommy can come help you pick some songs."

Owen jumped up with excitement and scurried off as fast as he could.

"What are you two up to?" Fallon asked.

Riley felt her face flush.

Andi shrugged. "Worried?"

"Should I be?" Fallon asked.

"Probably," Andi deadpanned.

"I'm going to go help Owen." Riley slid off her stool.

"Mommy!"

"I'm coming."

"What was that about?" Fallon asked.

"She knows, Fallon."

"She knows? What does she know?"

"About us."

"You told Riley?"

"I didn't tell her anything. She had it figured out."

Fallon groaned. *Great. She must think I'm a piece of shit now.*

"Relax," Andi said.

"Andi, Riley lost the love of her life. I doubt finding out we're having an affair exactly impressed her."

Andi shrugged. "She's not a wallflower, Fallon."

"What's the supposed to mean?"

"It means that you have her on some kind of pedestal. Be careful with that. Riley might be young, she's not as naïve as you seem to think."

"I don't think she's naïve."

Andi stared at Fallon doubtfully.

"I don't. I just… Me and Riley… I've told her a lot, Andi —not that."

"Why not?"

"Why not?" Fallon glanced over at Riley and Owen. "For one thing, I don't want everyone to know."

Andi raised an eyebrow.

"What?"

"Fallon, you and I both know that everyone in town knows about us. They ignore it."

Fallon bit her lip. Did everyone know? *Shit.* They probably did.

"What did she say?" Fallon asked.

"Just that she cares about you."

"She said that?"

She didn't have to. "Why does that surprise you?"

"It doesn't. It's been a while since anyone stuck around long enough to become a friend."

And, we're back to Liv. Andi nodded. "I'll be interested to hear what she thinks of Liv."

"You like her—Riley, I mean."

"What's not to like?" Andi asked.

"She's a good kid."

"She's not a kid, Fallon."

"You know what I mean!"

"I do. I wouldn't let her hear you say that."

Fallon groaned. "I just meant… She's not even thirty yet."

"Mm. She's lived more than a lot of people I know twice her age," Andi offered.

Yeah, I guess she has.

Andi finished her drink and hopped off her stool.

"You're leaving already?" Fallon asked.

"I am."

"Andi?"

"Yeah?"

"You seem… Did I do something to upset you?"

Andi reached over and took Fallon's hand. "No. I'll talk to you. Tell Liv I said hello."

"Hey," Fallon called after her lover.

Andi turned back.

Fallon's breath caught. She wasn't sure they had a name for what she felt. She would miss Andi while they had to be apart. She could call her. She would see her. She wouldn't hold her. And, as much as Fallon hated to admit it, she found comfort in Andi's arms.

Andi didn't need Fallon to utter a word. She winked. *I'll miss you too.*

Saturday

"Aunt Fallon?"

"What's up, Em?"

Emily looked up at Fallon and put her hands on her hips. Fallon had to bite her lip to keep from laughing. She'd seen the exact same expression on Oliva's face a million times. Emily reminded Fallon of Olivia more than Summer. They both had their mother's light brown skin and curly hair. Emily shared her mother's soft brown eyes. Summer's eyes were noticeably lighter, almost golden. She had little doubt that both would break their share of hearts when they got older. Emily possessed a sense of adventure where Summer tended to be timid. Fallon had learned that some parts of a person's personality started at birth. Emily had come into the world wide-eyed with wonder. Summer had always been more reserved. They were a blend of Olivia and Dean biologically. People could say anything they wanted; Fallon believed that both nature and nurture played a role in shaping a person. Looking at Emily, she felt confident in that assessment.

"I want the top bunk," Emily said.

Fallon nodded. "Let me guess; your sister wants it too."

"Yeah, but I'm older. She's too little."

"There you are," Olivia said. "Oh, I see. You think Fallon is going to take your side."

"Mom…"

"Don't Mom me. I told you to give your sister a chance."

"She'll fall!"

"She won't fall," Olivia said.

"Em," Fallon addressed her goddaughter. "You can take turns with your sister. You have a whole week."

"It's not fair!"

"Emily," Olivia warned.

The doorbell rang.

"I'll get that," Fallon said. She leaned into Olivia's ear. "She's yours."

"Don't remind me!" Olivia called after Fallon.

Fallon opened the door. "You didn't have to ring the bell," she told Riley. "You have a key."

Riley was about to answer when Owen spoke.

"Fawon!"

"Hi, Owen."

He held up his arms.

Fallon laughed. "Do I look like a bus?"

Owen laughed.

"I do," Fallon said. She picked up the toddler and led Riley through the door. "Welcome to the madness," she said.

Riley grinned. The noise level was certainly different than normal.

"Aunt Fallon!"

Fallon sighed. "Yes, Evan?"

"Can you hook up the Xbox for me and Em?"

"Yes, but you have to let Summer play too."

"Okay," he agreed.

"You want to help me, Owen?"

Owen nodded.

"Good, I need all the help I can get." She turned to Riley. "Let me introduce you to everyone. Evan," she called for her nephew's attention. "Em," she addressed Emily. "This is my friend, Riley," she said. "And, this is Owen."

Evan waved.

"Hi," Emily said.

"Hello," Riley replied.

"Where's your sister?" Fallon asked Emily.

"In the kitchen with Mom," Emily answered.

"Okay. I'll be back and I'll show you how to set up the game." Fallon led Riley to the kitchen. "Hey," she announced her presence.

Olivia turned and smiled. "This must be Riley."

"Nice to meet you," Riley said.

"And you. And, this is Owen?" Olivia guessed.

"Say hi, Owen," Fallon whispered.

Owen waved.

"This is my friend, Liv. And, that," she pointed to the little girl. "That is Summer."

Owen smiled.

"Do you want to go play with Summer?" Fallon asked. "She has some cool toys."

Owen nodded.

Fallon placed him on the ground. He held onto her leg and Riley's. Fallon chuckled. She'd never seen Owen act shy.

Riley crouched down to her son's height. "You can go with Summer, sweetheart. It's okay. Fallon and I will be right here."

Olivia watched Fallon and Riley with interest. Owen looked at his mother and then at Fallon for assurance. She wasn't surprised to see that Owen had bonded with Fallon. Fallon was a natural with children. That was one of the reasons Olivia had fallen in love with her. Having a family had always been important to Olivia. Finding someone she believed could fulfill her needs both as a woman and as a parent mattered to her in a partner. Fallon had fit the bill perfectly—almost perfectly.

"Go ahead, buddy," Fallon encouraged Owen. "You and Summer can play. I'll make you a hot dog later."

Owen grinned. "Hot dogs, Mommy!"

"So, I heard," Riley said. She grinned when Summer held out her hand for Owen and he accepted it. *That might be the cutest thing I've ever seen.*

"Can I get you a glass of wine or something before I go help the kids?" Fallon asked Riley.

"I've got it," Olivia said.

Fallon tried to smile. For some reason, she was not in love with the idea of leaving Olivia to entertain Riley.

Olivia folded her arms across her chest. "What is it? I promise, I won't get her drunk and take advantage of her," she said.

Fallon shouldn't have been surprised by Olivia's comment. She was.

"At least, I won't in the time it takes you to do whatever it is you are off to do," Olivia said.

Riley felt Fallon's discomfort. No matter how Riley tried to reassure her friend, it was clear that Fallon's concerns about her sexuality lingered. The people in Fallon's life were comfortable with who Fallon was. Riley was someone new. It was easy for her to understand why Fallon felt a degree of unease. She gently rubbed Fallon's back. "It'd take more wine than you have in this kitchen to manage that," Riley said. "But if Fallon's willing to drive me home, give it all you've got."

Fallon chuckled at the expression on Olivia's face. *Didn't see that one coming, did you, Liv?* "I'll leave you two to your debauchery."

"So," Olivia began. "Red or white?"

"Whatever does the trick," Riley said with a wink.

Olivia laughed. *Well, well, Riley, just who are you?* "Red it is."

❆ ❆ ❆

"No." Fallon held up a finger. "Em," she warned.

Bam! A snowball hit Fallon in the chest. Riley laughed. Owen had fallen asleep in Fallon's bed. Fallon had been lured outside by the porch lights for a snowball fight. It didn't take much to entice her outside. If ever Riley had witnessed a pathetic protest, it had been Fallon pretending that she had no desire to play in the snow. "I'm too old for the cold," she had said. Riley wondered if any of the kids had bought the theatrics for a second. She certainly hadn't.

"They'll be out here for a while," Olivia said. She closed the front door. "Coffee?"

"Sounds good," Riley replied.

"This is her winter game," Olivia commented. "Everything snow in the winter; everything water in the summer. I think she only wants kids so she can be one."

Riley smiled. She took notice of Olivia's wording and tone. She wondered if Olivia recalled the fact that she and Fallon were not a couple, and Emily and Summer were, in fact, children she shared with someone else. She liked Olivia. It was easy to see what had attracted Fallon to the woman. Beautiful seemed a deficient description for Olivia Nolan. Olivia looked more like a movie star to Riley than someone who worked for the government; unless she was playing a spy in the movies.

Not that it surprised her. Fallon was attractive and charismatic. People were drawn to her. It made sense that someone like Olivia would be charmed by Fallon, just as Fallon would find Olivia captivating. That was the word she had been searching for. Olivia was captivating. She was intelligent, articulate, and quick-witted; all things that enhanced her good looks. She also seemed possessive, or perhaps it was protective of Fallon.

"So, how long do you think you'll stay in Whiskey Springs?" Olivia inquired.

"I don't have any plans to leave."

"So, you plan to stay."

"To be honest, I haven't given much thought to it one way or the other. I needed a change."

"Fallon mentioned that you lost your husband. I'm sorry."

"Thank you. Yes, I did. It certainly wasn't in my plan," Riley said. She accepted a cup of coffee from Olivia. "Some things you can't plan for; they just happen."

"That they do," Olivia agreed. "Plans are a funny thing," she said. She looked out the window and sighed. "I'd like to think that we end up where we are meant to," she said as she turned her attention back to Riley.

"Destiny?" Riley asked.

"I don't believe in destiny, not one that's preordained anyway. I think we have choices that change our destiny."

Riley nodded. She had pondered destiny many times. It remained a difficult concept for her. She hadn't chosen Robert's death. He hadn't chosen it either. Someone had made a choice and turned her life upside down. A man chose to get in his car after a bender and he crashed into Robert. There was the choice. Robert was gone and she was alone because of another person's decision. Sometimes, you had no say in what happened to you. Life happened and you had to deal with it. If that wasn't destiny, what was it? What was the point to it if it wasn't preordained? It was a question with no answer. That's what Riley had come to believe. She had choices to make; that was true. Most of those choices had been thrust upon her. If Robert hadn't been on the road that day, she would be making different decisions.

"I suppose that's true," Riley said. "There are times when someone else's choice changes all of ours."

Olivia took a deep breath and let it out slowly. "You sound like Fallon."

Riley was curious.

"She says that to me all the time. My choice to leave changed her life."

"I'm sure it did," Riley offered honestly.

"It did. She forgets it was also her choice to stay. We're all affected by the decisions of other people. I still think it's how we respond to those decisions that shape our destiny."

"Maybe," Riley said. "All I know is that life goes on even when you sometimes wish it wouldn't."

"Loss is hard."

"Yes, it is," Riley said.

"It gets better."

"It does," Riley agreed. "But it never completely goes away."

Olivia glanced out the window again. "No, it doesn't."

"Do you miss it?" Riley asked. "Living here, I mean?"

Olivia smiled. "Sometimes, I do. It wasn't the right place for me. Fallon could never understand that."

"She loves this place."

"She does. It's her home," Olivia said. "She fits here."

"You didn't?"

"As much as I could, I did. I wasn't so sure our kids would."

Riley was taken aback by the comment. Whiskey Springs was a friendly town. She was sure that there were plenty of skeletons in people's closets, and Riley had heard her share of gossip in the last month. People were people no matter where you traveled. She wouldn't hesitate to raise children here.

"I know what you're thinking—small town, nice people, safe, quiet. It's all those things," Olivia said. "It's not…"

"A hub for culture?" Riley guessed. She meant no offense. Small-town life differed from city life, and Olivia lived in a city. In places like San Diego and Washington DC there were gallery openings, film screenings, plays, wine tastings, museum exhibitions, and political roundtables to attend every day of the week. You could find all those things in Vermont, but events were scattered and far less frequent. Whiskey Springs offered karaoke on Thursdays at The VFW and movie night every Friday at the small library. The town did take great pride in its fire museum and the historical society it boasted. It was not the city.

Olivia chuckled. "There is that. It also lacks diversity," she said honestly.

That was a concept Riley understood. She'd seen the evidence of its impact on Fallon. There was no LGBT center, and there was a notable lack of color in the town. There was one couple from Mexico, and Fallon had introduced Riley to Mr. Okada. He was a World War II veteran whose son occasionally brought him into *Murphy's Law* when he visited. That was it. Olivia's observation was not just candid, it was personal.

"I've noticed," Riley said.

"I'm not surprised. Coming from a city, it's more noticeable."

Riley nodded.

Olivia sipped her wine. "When it came time for this house to be completed—I don't know; I felt it all press in on me," she said with a sigh. "We'd always said that I would carry our children. That was never a burning desire for Fallon—the pregnancy part."

Olivia couldn't begin to explain why she was sharing all of this with Riley. She barely knew the woman. She did know that Riley had become important to Fallon. She'd witnessed the evidence of that all afternoon. If Riley mattered to Fallon, Riley mattered to Olivia. Fallon would always be a central part of Olivia's life. It might not be the way she had once hoped, but Fallon still meant the world to Olivia. And, she imagined that Fallon told their story somewhat differently. No matter how many times they argued, no matter how many ways Olivia sought to explain why she felt the need to leave, Fallon could never seem to accept Olivia's feelings. Whiskey Springs was home to Fallon. It had always been her home and Olivia knew that it always would be. Was she seeking Riley's approval? Maybe she was hoping Riley would grant her the absolution she still craved. One thing that Oliva felt certain about; Riley Main wasn't about to disappear anytime soon.

"Anyway," Olivia continued. "Fallon always wanted kids. It's one of the many things we had in common."

Riley smiled.

"Our kids would hardly look like their schoolmates. There were days, Riley; there were days when I wondered who was looking at me. I mean, here I was a black lesbian in a town where there was one other lesbian—the one I lived with, and not a single person of color except me. I didn't want my kids to grow up that way."

Riley wasn't sure what to say. She'd be lying if she claimed that she couldn't see Olivia's point. She also knew that Olivia's departure had hurt Fallon deeply. She wondered why Olivia had wanted to build a house, build a life with Fallon in a place that felt so foreign to her. It seemed obvious that Olivia carried both guilt and some amount of regret. Riley wasn't sure what the latter was about—leaving Fallon or agreeing to start a family with her in the first place. "Do you wish you had stayed?"

"No," Olivia answered without hesitation. "I wish I hadn't hurt her so badly. Don't get me wrong; it hurt me too. It was my decision. I think somehow that made it a little easier for me. I wanted her to come. The truth is; it wouldn't have worked. She would've resented me in the end."

"Not an easy road," Riley said.

"No."

"You came out friends."

"We did."

"You still love her," Riley surmised.

"I'll always love her. I think if you love someone from your soul, you always love them. It changes. I love Barb. That doesn't take anything away from what Fallon and I shared."

"I understand."

"I'm sure you do. What about you? Whiskey Springs isn't exactly the hot bed for dating," Olivia said.

Riley laughed. "I haven't even thought about that."

"Not ready?"

"I don't know that I'd say that. I'm not avoiding it," Riley said. "I'm not about to start signing up for Match.com either. Someday—someday, I hope there will be someone again."

Olivia smiled. Riley was engaging. She possessed the unique ability to set people at ease immediately. Olivia wasn't surprised that Fallon had gravitated to the younger woman. Riley's light-hearted sense of humor was infectious and genuine. In a few hours, she'd managed to capture the attention of all three children. She was content to listen, but when she spoke all eyes turned to her. Down to earth and unassuming seemed to be Riley's nature. It said a great deal about the woman standing in the kitchen Olivia had once called hers. The mark that loss left on a person often reflected cynicism and rigidity. Neither was evident in Riley's demeanor. In fact, the young woman seemed to Olivia to be naturally trusting and optimistic. *No wonder Fallon is enthralled.*

Fallon jogged into the kitchen out of breath.

Riley smirked. Fallon was a mess. Her hair was sticking out from underneath her hat at peculiar angles. Her jacket and pants seemed to have been pelted by as much dirt as snow. A trail of mud traced her footsteps from the door to the kitchen.

"Please tell me the children are cleaner than you," Olivia said.

"They're on their way to the bathroom," Fallon said. "Evan will use mine."

"And, the girls?" Olivia asked.

"I've got it," Fallon said.

Olivia rolled her eyes. "I'll handle it. I hope I see you again soon," she told Riley.

"Me too," Riley replied. She looked at Fallon and shook her head.

"What?" Fallon asked.

"Who won?" Riley asked.

"Me, of course!"

"Of course," Riley said.

"You don't believe me?"

Olivia groaned in the distance. "You have some laundry to do!" she yelled to Fallon.

Fallon grinned. "Good thing I have laundry service."

"Oh no, not yet, you don't," Riley reminded her.

"You still think you can win this bet?" Fallon asked.

"I told you; I like my odds."

Fallon shrugged. "I like snowball fights."

Riley poked her cheek with her tongue. She did not miss Fallon's meaning. Fallon was determined to win their bet, and if she had her way, Riley suspected she'd be facing a pile of muddy laundry next week. "We'll see, Foster. We'll see."

Fallon winked. "I'll stock up on Tide."

Riley laughed. *I'm sure you will.*

CHAPTER SEVEN

March 15th

"Are you seriously still doing her laundry?" Carol asked.

"My last week of servitude," Riley said. "I still can't believe I lost."

Riley laughed as she hoisted Owen onto her hip. When Fallon set her mind to something, she did it. Riley had been given that lesson in spades. She'd done more laundry than she had ever imagined in the last month. Fallon had attempted to let her off the hook more than once, but Riley insisted that she make good on their wager. A bet was a bet, and Riley was good for her word. Doing Fallon's laundry also gave her a reason to see her friend, not that she needed one. They had a standing dinner date twice a week—every Monday and every Thursday night. They'd yet to miss one. Riley looked forward to her evenings with Fallon. Some nights they talked for hours, sharing stories about college and even their "first time." Other evenings, they found themselves in front of the television watching some crazy action movie or indulging in a few episodes of *The X-Files* or *Friends*. Fallon loved *Friends*. She would recite the lines before they were spoken. It amused Riley endlessly. Of course, there was the one time that Fallon convinced Riley they needed to watch *Super Why* with Owen because Owen had a cold and needed to rest. Fallon had quickly become her best friend. Riley reveled in their relationship.

Carol pushed opened Riley's front door.

"Thanks," Riley said.

"Thanks for lunch," Carol said.

"My pleasure." Owen fought Riley's grasp. She put him down and removed his jacket and shoes. "Go ahead and play, sweetheart."

"He certainly is full of energy."

"Yes, he is," Riley agreed.

"Mommy! I Swed!"

"Swed?" Carol asked.

"Sled," Riley clarified. She wondered if Fallon was secretly grooming Owen for a future in bobsledding. Riley's backyard sported a small hill. It didn't seem to matter whether two inches or ten inches of snow blanketed it; Fallon had Owen in his sled—a sled that Fallon had purchased. Dwindling snow coverage did nothing to deter Owen and Fallon's enthusiasm for sledding. She chuckled. "Every time she's here, she's got him out in that sled."

"Sounds like Fallon. She's a big kid."

"So, I've noticed. She loves to ski."

"She does," Carol agreed.

"She doesn't go often. The last time she went the kids were here."

Carol shrugged. "Yeah, she sort of slowed down after she broke her ankle."

"She broke it skiing?"

"No, she broke it walking through the parking lot at the pub."

"How?"

"Who knows?" Carol shrugged again. "She was out of the pub for a few days."

"She worked with a broken ankle?"

Another shrug served as Carol's reply.

"God, she's stubborn."

"You think?" Carol laughed. "What are you two up to tonight?"

"Other than me cooking dinner? Who knows? Mud sledding?"

"Wouldn't surprise me."

"Me neither. I think she wants to torture me with the dirtiest laundry possible until the last minute."

Carol laughed. "Sorry," she apologized when her phone rang. "Hey, Ida. What?"

Riley watched as Carol's face drained of all color.

"What happened? No, of course I can. Don has to leave by four; I know. No, I'm at Riley's." Carol looked at Riley and sighed. "Yeah, I'll tell her. Is she okay? I'll bet she is. Don't sweat it."

Riley's heart dropped. *Is who okay?*

Carol looked at Riley. "Do you want to talk to her?" Carol held the phone out for Riley. "It's Ida."

Riley took the phone nervously. "Ida."

"Now, before you go getting all upset, you listen to me."

"Okay."

"Fallon had a little car accident."

Riley held her breath. Accident was a word that conjured images that made Riley's stomach revolt.

"Some idiot tried to pass her, ran her right off the road."

"How bad?"

"The car is totaled. Fallon will survive." Ida heard Riley's breath catch. "She's okay, Riley. More annoyed than anything else."

"Where are you?"

"UVMC in Essex."

Riley forced herself to breathe. *She's fine. Relax, Riley.*

"Riley?"

"I'm here."

"I was wondering if you could do me a favor," Ida said.

"Whatever you need."

"Do you think I could deposit Her Highness with you for the night? She's supposed to rest and stay off her feet. I'm supposed to head to Albany tomorrow morning. She'll never forgive me if I cancel."

"Of course," Riley said. "Do you need me to come there?"

"No. She's signing paperwork now. I should be there within the hour."

"I'll be here." Riley handed the phone back to Carol.

"You okay?" Carol asked.

Riley nodded. *Not even a little bit.* She vividly recalled the troopers at her door after Robert's accident. It took her two weeks to get the courage to sit behind the wheel of her car, and much longer to stop anticipating disaster at every turn. She never wanted to hear the words car and accident in the same sentence again, and she wasn't sure she'd ever consider any incident "little."

"Hey, look at the bright side." Carol tried to lighten Riley's mood. "At least she won't be playing in the mud tonight."

Riley smiled. It was a smile devoid of amusement. She felt sick, and she was positive nothing but seeing Fallon walk through her door would quell the anxiety creeping through her bones. "There is that," she confessed.

※　※　※

Riley opened the front door and took the first full breath she had in an hour. *She's okay.*

"Good luck," Ida said as she helped Fallon to the door.

"I can walk, Mom," Fallon grumbled.

Riley smiled. "So, it would appear."

"Well, I'm happy you can walk, Fallon," Ida said. "You do have three broken ribs and a mild concussion. So, do us all a favor and behave."

"I feel fine." Fallon grimaced as she took a seat on Riley's sofa.

Riley shook her head.

"Fawon!" Owen ran into the room.

"Owen," Riley warned. "Gentle. You need to be gentle with Fallon. She has some boo boos."

Owen looked at Fallon sheepishly. She had a bruise on her forehead and a small cut over her right eye.

Fallon reached down for him.

"Fallon," Riley and Ida cautioned in unison.

Fallon ignored them. She winced as she picked Owen up and placed him on her lap.

Stubborn. Riley wanted to scream. Her nerves were still frayed.

"Boo boo?" Owen touched Fallon's forehead.

"Just a little one." She smiled at Owen.

"Fawon, swed?"

"No sledding," Riley said firmly.

Fallon groaned.

Ida chuckled. *Met your match, Fallon.* "Don't be afraid to put her in time-out," Ida said.

Riley nodded.

"And, you." Ida pointed at Fallon. "You behave. No work tomorrow, Fallon."

"Mom, I'm fine."

"You're deluded, is what you are. Don't give Riley any trouble. I mean it."

"What are you going to do, ground me?" Fallon replied.

"Watch me," Ida said. She'd nearly had a heart attack when she got the call that Fallon was on way to the hospital in an ambulance. She still hadn't managed to calm the shaking in her hands. She was determined to conceal that from both her daughter and Riley.

Ida had lost her brother in a car crash. He had just turned twenty. She had never taken a drive lightly again. She suspected that the same held true for Riley. That understanding is what prompted her to suggest Fallon spend the night at Riley's home. That, and the fact that she was curious about the relationship between her daughter and Riley Main. She was aware that Fallon continued to see Andi. And, while it might have surprised most people, Ida had no issue with the affair. Andi and Fallon had been friends for years. Jake Maguire was a notable philanderer. Andi was lonely. Fallon was lonely. Fallon was also timid when it came to romantic entanglements. Ida wished that her daughter would open herself to the possibility of a new relationship. She suspected that Fallon's feelings for Riley ran deeper than friendship. Whether either Riley or Fallon realized that, she couldn't be sure. And, she had no idea how either might react to that reality. This much was evident to Ida: Fallon and Riley cared deeply for each other. Whatever path their friendship followed, Ida felt confident the friendship would endure.

"I'm sorry I have to drop her off and leave."

"Don't be," Riley said. "I'll make her behave."

Ida smiled. "I have no doubt." She hugged Riley.

"Be careful driving to Albany," Riley said.

"I will be."

Riley let Ida out and sucked in a deep breath. She walked into the living room to find Fallon sitting with her eyes closed, Owen looking at her curiously. "Owen, why don't you go get your bear and you and Fallon can watch that movie you like while I make dinner?"

Owen looked at his mother fearfully and then back at Fallon.

Fallon opened one eye. "*Super Why,* buddy," she said. "I'll be right here." She closed her eyes again.

Owen climbed off the couch and toddled toward his room.

"How are you feeling?" Riley asked.

"I'm fine."

Riley doubted that. "Did you call Andi yet?"

Fallon opened her eyes. "Why would I do that? She and Jake are in Florida with the boys."

"I know that."

"She doesn't need to hear from me."

Riley sighed. *Yes, she does.* "Fallon, she's going to hear. You know I'm right. You don't think Pete or Carol is going to text her?"

Fallon huffed.

"She cares about you. Don't let her hear it from them, and don't let her worry."

"I'm fine," Fallon snapped. Her heart skipped when she saw tears brimming in Riley's eyes. *Shit. Way to go, Fallon.* "Riley? Why are you so upset?"

Riley shook her head.

"Come over here."

"I need to start dinner."

"Come over here," Fallon said.

Riley complied reluctantly.

"What's got you so upset?" Fallon asked.

"What's got me so upset? Fallon." She tenderly touched the cut over Fallon's eye. "You could've been killed," she whispered hoarsely.

"I'm okay. Riley, look at me."

Riley couldn't meet Fallon's gaze. It might have been irrational, but she couldn't stop the way she felt.

Fallon, you idiot. "Hey," Fallon coaxed Riley to open her eyes. "I'm sorry."

"Why are you sorry? I'm the one acting like a baby."

"No, you aren't. I wasn't thinking. I can be a first-class asshole sometimes."

"No…"

"Oh, yes, I can. I wasn't thinking about you or Mom; how you would feel getting that call. I just wanted to get home."

"You're my best friend, Fallon. I don't want to think about losing you too."

Fallon pulled Riley into her arms. "I'm sorry."

Riley cried. She cried with relief. She remembered the day Robert died. She cried for the loss. She cried, and she cried some more. Fallon held her, and she let herself cry.

Owen walked into the room dragging his bear by the arm. Fallon smiled at him. "Come up here, buddy."

"Mommy."

Riley pulled away from Fallon slightly, wiped her eyes, and smiled at her son. "Let me put in that movie for you."

Fallon pulled her back onto the sofa. "Thank you for caring," she whispered.

I do care. Riley nodded.

"I'll call Andi."

"Good." Riley gathered herself and made her way to the kitchen. She gripped the counter. *What would I do if something happened to her?* She pushed the thought from her mind. Fallon was safe. Everyone was safe. *Dinner, Riley.*

❧ ❧ ❧

Riley picked up her phone. "Hi, Andi."

"How are you holding up?" Andi asked.

"Me?"

"Yes, you."

"I'm fine. I take it she called you."

"She did. Thanks for that."

"No problem."

"Seriously, how are you?" Andi asked.

"I'm okay. You know Fallon; she thinks she should be up doing something—anything."

"Sounds about right. How are *you*?"

Riley sighed.

"That's what I thought."

"It's the call; you know?"

"I think I can imagine," Andi said.

Fallon had called Andi while Riley went to make dinner. She'd confessed that she felt horrible for not thinking about how her mother and Riley must have felt. Both had lost someone they loved in a car wreck, and Fallon's car was wrecked. She confided to Andi that she knew she was lucky. Someone had been watching over her. She hadn't told either her mother or Riley how hard she had hit the tree. In fact, she hadn't mentioned the tree at all. She'd seen people hospitalized or killed from softer collisions. Fallon's admissions had taken Andi's breath away for a moment. Andi was and always would be the person that Fallon could tell anything to—anything at all. Andi would never pass judgement and she was capable of handling the truth. That didn't change the fact that the truth left Andi rattled.

"I'm glad she called you," Riley said.

"I'm glad she's with you." *I am. It's strange, but I am.*

Riley wasn't sure what to say. "How's the visit going?"

"Good." Andi brightened. "Jacob took me to this restaurant he and his friends love last night. Jake and Dave went to a movie. I can't remember the last time it was just Jacob and me. It was fun. I can't believe he's twenty-one. My kid bought me a drink."

Riley laughed. Andi adored her sons. Motherhood was a bond that she shared with Andi. She loved to hear Andi talk about her boys. She seemed to glow with pride whenever she had the chance to tell a story about one of them. Riley also understood that Andi missed them sorely. She accepted that Andi loved her husband and family. Secretly, she wondered if Andi might be happier with someone who was present in her life on a daily basis. She valued all the friendships she had made since arriving in town, but she remained closest to Andi and Fallon. She hoped that if their affair ever came to an end, that she would be able to maintain the closeness she shared with them both.

"Sounds like a fun trip."

"It has been. Are you sure you're okay? I know that call had to shake you up."

"It did. Don't ever tell her I told you this; she fell asleep a while ago. I checked to see if she was breathing twice."

Andi listened. *Oh, Riley, how is it that you don't see it?* "Be glad she's sleeping."

"I know. I should be."

"Listen, thanks for making her call. Carol texted me about ten minutes after she called."

I knew it. "No problem. See you next week?"

"With a tan," Andi said. "I didn't even have to get sprayed!"

Riley laughed. "Color me jealous." Riley burned under a sixty-watt light bulb. Dark hair and eyes did not equate to golden brown skin.

"Call if you need to talk," Andi said.

"I won't."

Andi laughed.

"Call, I mean."

"I'll see you soon, Riley."

Riley put her phone on the counter. *Now, if I can keep Fallon quiet for the next twenty-four hours...*

CHAPTER EIGHT

April 5th

Riley wondered if Carol had any idea what Charlie was planning, or rather what Fallon had planned for him. One of the only ways Riley had managed to convince Fallon to stay home for a few days after her accident had been promising that she would go shopping with Charlie for Carol's engagement ring.

"I have things I need to do," Fallon argued.

"What things?" Riley challenged.

"Carol's party is only a few weeks away."

"And?"

"What do you mean, and? And, I have to make sure everything is set."

"Why do you need to be at work to do that?"

"You need space. You need to work," Fallon said. "You can't be waiting on me."

"It's not as if I am potty-training you too."

"Funny."

"Fallon, you need to take a few days."

"I feel fine."

"You won't feel fine if you push it too soon," Riley reminded her.

Fallon groaned. "Charlie wants me to help him shop."

Riley chuckled. "For what?"

"A ring."

"A ring?"

"Yeah, for Carol. What do I know about that?"

Riley decided not to remind Fallon that she had once purchased a ring for Olivia. She suspected that was part of what was driving Fallon's attitude. Planning a party was one thing. Charlie was a sweetheart. He was caring for an aging mother with dementia and running a business. Riley was sure that Fallon had offered more than Charlie had requested her help. Rings were something of a different order than parties. Rings reminded Fallon of Olivia. Sitting still had Fallon pondering all kinds of things, not the least of which was getting herself anxious about shopping with Charlie.

"I told you a long time ago that I would help you any way I could," Riley said.

Fallon sighed.

"What if I go with Charlie? Do you think you can handle watching Owen for an afternoon?"

Fallon's eyes brightened. *"You'll go with him?"*

"Sure. I like sparkly things."

"Are you sure?" Fallon had been reluctant to ask Riley. Would looking for engagement rings remind Riley of what she'd lost? She had even considered asking Andi to take Charlie.

Riley guessed where Fallon's thoughts had traveled. *"I'll be fine,"* she said. *"I'd like to think that maybe someday, someone will buy me something sparkling again."*

Fallon was surprised by Riley's admission. *"I've no doubt."*

"Maybe. So, do we have a deal?"

"You want to make another deal with me?" Fallon teased.

"A deal, not a bet."

Fallon laughed.

"You can tie up what you need to from home. You stay off your feet for the next couple of days like the doctor suggested. I'll take Charlie shopping."

"How many days?"

"Fallon…"

"Okay! Anything to get out of shopping."

"What do you think?" Charlie asked.

Riley looked at the ring on the counter. It was stunning, neither overstated nor diminutive. It was elegant. "I think it's perfect."

"Really?"

"Really," Riley promised.

"I hope they have a return policy," he muttered.

"She's not going to say no."

Charlie looked at Riley hopefully.

Riley squeezed his arm. "She's crazy about you."

"You think so?"

"I know so."

Charlie exhaled with relief. "I'll take it," he told the clerk.

"How does it feel?" Riley wondered.

"What?"

"I don't know, I've never bought anyone an engagement ring."

"Yeah, but you've been given one."

"True."

"What was it like for you?"

Riley giggled. "A bit less than romantic."

"Why?"

"Well, we were in the mall and he turned to me and said, 'I think we should by a ring.' I thought he was joking until he pulled me into a jewelry store."

"You're kidding?"

"No, I swear."

"You said yes, though."

"Actually, he never asked the question." Riley laughed. "I picked out a ring. He bought it. He put it on my finger. That was it. We were married a year later."

"Wow."

Riley smiled. "I wouldn't change one minute."

"Really?"

Riley nodded.

"You must miss him."

"I do."

"Sorry if this was…"

Riley took Charlie's arm again. "This was fun," she said. "I'm happy for you and Carol."

"If she says yes."

"She'd be a fool not to."

Charlie finished his transaction. "What about you?"

"Me?"

"Yeah, think you'll ever do it again?"

"Get married?" Riley asked.

"Yeah."

"I don't know. I hope so."

"You know, Jerry's been asking about you."

"Jerry?"

"Yeah. Jerry Walker, you know; the roof guy."

Riley smiled. "I know who Jerry is."

"I think he's kind of sweet on you."

Riley's eyebrow raised. *Jerry?* "What makes you think that?"

"He just asks about you a lot is all," Charlie explained.

"Hum." Riley had run into Jerry a handful of times. He seemed friendly. She had to admit she hadn't given much thought to Jerry at all, and certainly not romantically. Then again, Riley hadn't indulged in romantic fantasies of any kind since Robert's death. Jerry Walker? She shook off the thought.

"He's a good guy, Riley."

Riley's only response was a smile. *I'm sure he is.*

⋇   ⋇   ⋇

Fallon watched as Ida and Andi put the finishing touches on the tables at the pub. She wondered for the zillionth time how she managed to get herself volunteered for these things. Andi had suggested that she volunteered herself. Ida agreed. *Figures.* Maybe she did offer to help Charlie. Maybe she offered her assistance too freely at times. Why shouldn't she? Ida was independent. Fallon didn't have aging parents, young children, or a significant other to care for. She functioned on her timetable. She could afford to hire more staff at *Murphy's Law,* something both Andi and her mother had advised her to do on countless occasions. Why should she? What would she do if she were home? Fallon wasn't a TV junkie. Okay, so maybe she had a slight addiction to sitcoms and thriller movies. A person could only sit in front of a screen for so long. She had chopped enough firewood to last her two winters, maybe three. She couldn't exactly immerse herself in gardening during the winter; not that she would choose to. What did people do when they had no one to go home to? In Fallon's experience they got a hobby, took a lover or went to the pub. In her case, she had done all three. Immersing herself in her friends' projects and problems was her hobby, Andi was her lover, and she owned a pub. She'd made that argument to Riley.

"So, this is your hobby?" Riley asked.

"Yeah."

"Fallon, usually people choose hobbies that they enjoy."

"What do you mean?"

"You've been groaning about this party for months now."

"Riley, you been here a while."

"And?"

"There's a couple of things about living in a small town that I would have thought you would've caught onto by now."

"Such as?"

"The three g's."

"The three g's?"

"Yep. The gift of gab, the ability to gossip, and something to grumble about."

Riley laughed. "I see, so it's a prerequisite then?"
"Exactly."
"I'll work on that."
"See that you do."

"Are you going to help or just stand there daydreaming?" Ida asked.

"Huh?"

"You. Should Andi and I expect a paycheck?" Ida asked.

Fallon leaned against the bar. "When was the last time either one of you paid for a drink?"

"I think we've both paid plenty," Ida said. "Andi?"

Andi laughed.

"Hey," Riley tried to open the door while holding an armload of bags.

Fallon rushed over to help. Andi and Ida exchanged an amused glance.

"Thanks," Riley said.

"Why didn't you call? I would've come over and picked you up? How much is in the car?" Fallon took some bags from her hand and set them aside.

"Do you see that?" Ida asked Andi.

Andi smiled. *Oh, I see it.*

"Hi," Riley greeted Ida and Andi.

"Do you need some help?" Andi asked.

"I've got it," Fallon said and promptly followed Riley out the door.

Ida rolled her eyes. "That's it; I'm fixing a drink. Andi?"

"Are you buying too?" Andi asked.

"Hell, I paid for her first car and her college education. She can spring for the tequila." She stepped behind the bar.

"What are you doing?" Fallon asked when she stepped back inside.

"What does it look like I'm doing?" Ida replied. "Andi and I have been your flunkies for the last two hours. It's a birthday party, Fallon. I'm ready for the party to start."

Riley chuckled. "What do you still need to do?"

"Nothing," Fallon admitted quietly. "I just like to watch her pretend she's wounded. Watch, she'll tell Andi she raised me to respect my elders, not to enslave them."

Riley chanced a glance at Ida and Andi. She could hear those words falling from Ida's lips. The dynamic between Andi and Ida surprised her at times. Ida was aware that Fallon and Andi were lovers. She seemed to accept the situation without any judgment at all. Why that surprised Riley, she couldn't say. How would she feel if Owen one day found himself involved with a married woman? *Thank God, I don't have to worry about that for years.* Most people were raised to believe certain things, brought up with expectations about life and taught to stay within set boundaries. Whatever existed between Fallon and Andi fell outside all those things yet everyone seemed to accept it without hesitation. Was it because they weren't *in love* as Andi had suggested? From where Riley stood it appeared that a fine line existed between loving a person and being in love with them. She wondered how a person knew the difference. How had she known that she was i*n love* with Robert? Was it the attraction she felt to him, their physical connection? Was it the flutter in her stomach and the longing she felt when they parted? And, why did seeing Andi and Fallon together make her ponder all these things? Maybe it was the day ahead. Charlie and Carol would leave the party as an engaged couple. Fallon would likely leave with Andi. She would leave alone—again.

"You okay?" Fallon grabbed Riley's arm.

"Huh?"

"You were in another world there for a minute."

"Sorry. Just thinking." Riley smiled. "Do they know?" She gestured to Ida and Andi who were laughing together at the bar.

"That Charlie's going to propose?"

Riley nodded.

"Andi does."

"You tell her everything, don't you?"

Not everything. "Most things, I guess," Fallon replied.

Fallon's eyes fell on Andi. *Most things.* Riley had become Fallon's best friend. Sometimes you got more than one best friend. People played different roles in life. Andi was far more than a lover to Fallon. She couldn't deny that their physical relationship had brought them closer as friends. She imagined that most people would find that strange. Lovers were meant to be lovers, not friends. Friendship inevitably led to strings attached. Andi had been her friend long before their lips had met. She trusted Andi, perhaps more than she had ever trusted another person—save Ida. One thing Fallon did know, Andi Maguire would never hurt her if she could prevent it. She accepted Fallon as she was with all her flaws and all her fears. Fallon wouldn't admit it to anyone, but Andi understood her better than anyone. Their future would never entail romantic trips or heartfelt proposals. It was founded on affection, respect, and attraction. Fallon recognized the questions in Riley's eyes.

Riley had been in love once. She confessed to Fallon during one of their late-night conversations that she wondered if love could endure. Fallon had answered honestly. She shared the same questions as Riley. She guessed that everyone did. Romance novels and movies promised one great love—a soulmate that would complete you and suddenly make everything right. Every question would be answered in one kiss, and you could live happily ever after without questions, fears, or doubt. That seemed unrealistic to Fallon. Every person felt fear. Every person struggled with insecurity. In her experience, love and friendship were guides. A person could offer comfort, solace, even insight; no person could make another suddenly complete. And, as far as Fallon was concerned loving someone—

no matter how much—would never ensure perfection. Too often, she thought, the search for that one perfect, happy ending led people astray. Love came without warning. Relationships took work.

"Sometimes I wonder if it's possible to fall in love and have it last," Riley said.

"Why would you say that?"

"This will sound awful."

"I doubt that," Fallon said.

"Look around us. My parents, Andi, you and Liv… me—does it last—ever?" Riley sighed. *"I lost Robert. I thought it might kill me. I can't imagine losing him to someone else. Sometimes I wonder if he had lived, if we made it another ten or twenty years together, would he still love me—only me? In some ways, I think losing him to someone else would hurt even more."*

Fallon took a deep breath.

"You don't agree?"

"I didn't say that," Fallon replied. *"I don't think we get to choose who we love. I'm not sure we get much of a say in how they leave either. You don't decide to fall in love with someone, Riley. I don't think so. It just happens."* Fallon chuckled. *"And when it does it usually comes out of nowhere, or at least it seems that way. I can understand what you're saying. You lost the person you fell in love with too soon. Who knows what would have happened? I'm no expert on relationships. Look at my life. I do believe you can love more than one person. It's never the same, though. Every person is different so there's no way you can love them the same way. Like I said, I don't think love is a choice. How we love is. What kind of relationship—if we want to have a relationship at all with someone, that's our choice; loving someone isn't."*

Fallon smiled at Riley. "Weird, huh?"

"What?"

"My mom and Andi. That's what you were thinking."

Riley sighed. *Caught.* "Not weird, just…"

"Weird." Fallon laughed. "I guess most people would expect a parent's disapproval. Mom loves Andi as much as I do."

"Do you? Love her?" *Why are you asking her that—here of all places?*

Fallon smiled. "Yes."

Riley nodded.

"But what we have is what we have," Fallon said. "It won't last forever."

"Then why…"

"Why does anyone do anything they do? Who knows? Maybe we just needed someone at the same time."

Riley smiled. She watched Fallon approach the two women at the bar and considered Fallon's words. Fallon's explanation made sense. She felt a twinge of jealousy. It had been almost two years since Riley had experienced feeling another person close. A small part of her felt guilty for the feelings that were beginning to resurface in her, the needs of a woman. She would turn thirty in a couple of weeks. Her whole life was still ahead of her, however long that turned out to be. Would she spend it alone? Would she ever love someone as much as she had Robert? Could she let herself love another person? She'd promised him forever. Forever, what a cruel joke. She wasn't sure she wanted to be in love. Being in love carried the potential for heartbreak. Sex? Riley missed sex. Could she take a lover—just a lover? She had a few times before she met Robert. Her first two years of college had been an exercise in exploration. She'd told him enough. She'd never told him all of it. Oddly, it was Andi she had confided in about her past and her feelings. She seemed to confide nearly everything to Andi. It was a little strange when she thought about it. Riley spent long hours with Fallon. She had told Fallon a bit about her college days. She did not tell Fallon that she was feeling frustrated and thinking about those days lately. She never wanted to lose Fallon's friendship. She loved their banter and their long talks. Still, she held back parts of herself with Fallon. The contrast left her wondering who Andi was to her. Riley's thoughts traveled to the lunch she had shared with Andi earlier that week.

"Something's bothering you," Andi observed.

Riley shrugged.

"Riley?"

"It will sound… I don't know. I don't want you to think that I'm some kind of horny slut."

Andi erupted in laughter. "You're worried about me thinking you're a slut?" She laughed some more.

"I'm serious."

"You do realize who you are talking to."

"I don't see you that way," Riley said. "At all."

"Good to know." Andi smiled at her friend. "Let me guess, you're feeling a little frustrated?"

"More than a little. Pete was flirting with me at the pub the other night and for a second I considered pulling him into the bathroom."

Andi laughed. "That is some frustration."

"I know! What is wrong with me?"

"Nothing," Andi said.

"It doesn't feel that way."

"Can I ask you something?"

"Why not? I can't believe I just admitted that."

"That you're horny enough to fuck Pete?"

Riley shuddered. "It passed quickly."

"I'm sure. Why does it bother you? Is it because of Robert?"

Riley sighed. "Maybe. I haven't been with anyone else since I was twenty-one."

Andi smiled.

"I guess I never thought I'd have to think about it again."

"Being with someone new?" Andi guessed.

Riley nodded.

"I understand that."

"You do?"

"Sure, I do. I met Jake when I was nineteen. He was the only person to touch me for twenty-five years."

"Did you ever think about it? I mean, before you and Fallon…"

"Being with someone else?" Andi asked.

"Yeah."

"Of course."

"Really?"

"Not right away, and I never acted on it until…"

"Fallon."

Andi nodded. "Yes. I wish I could tell you that I regret it. I don't."

"I'm not sure I would even know what to do now."

Andi chuckled. "Somehow, I think you'll be fine."

"Maybe. It's not like I was never adventurous. Don't you think it's strange?"

"What's that?"

"I'm not lying awake thinking about Robert. I mean, I do. But when I think about…"

"Sex?"

"Yeah. I don't know; I think about college."

"When you were adventurous?"

"I guess. More like uninhibited."

Andi smiled broadly. "I don't think it's strange at all."

"It's not like I want to go out and have a one-night stand."

"Unless it's throwing Pete against the bathroom wall," Andi teased.

"Oh, God." Riley groaned. "It was one-second. Less than one-second."

"That's probably how long it would have lasted too," Andi joked.

"Please, forget I mentioned that."

Andi chuckled.

"Robert… Our relationship was great—in the bedroom, I mean. It wasn't timid." Riley blushed. "We never talked about the details of our past. I know he was with people. He knew that I wasn't exactly chaste."

Andi's eyebrow raised.

"I had a couple of boyfriends before we met. I had a few—experiences."

Andi was curious.

Riley smirked. "I know what you're wondering. Yes, I've been with a woman."

Andi nodded. "And?"

"I have no regrets," Riley replied. "About any of the people I've been with. I just… Part of me wants to find a bar, find a boy…"

"Or a girl?"

"At this point, I think human is negotiable."

Andi chuckled. "So, what's holding you back?"

"That's the thing; I don't know. Robert. Some of it is Robert."

"But not all of it."

Riley shook her head. "I don't know." She didn't. There was some unseen force gripping her.

Andi reached across the table and squeezed Riley's hand. "When it's the right moment and the right person, you'll know."

"I don't know. What if I forgot how?"

Andi's laughter filled the room. Riley was adorable. "It'll come back to you."

A sudden realization hit her. Who had Andi become in her life? Andi turned and looked at Riley curiously. Riley smiled warmly. She loved her big sister, Mary. Their relationship challenged her at times. Mary was not the person she chose to confide her deepest secrets and desires to; that person was Andi. *Big sister.* Andi's unspoken question was evident to Riley. She put her arm around Andi's shoulder. She couldn't explain why, but she'd been feeling nervous all morning. Her thoughts and her feelings were spiraling. Andi's presence comforted her.

"Oh, good, you're all here." Charlie burst through the door.

Fallon looked at him curiously. "Aren't you supposed to be getting ready for this party you made me plan?"

"Yeah. Yeah, I am." He looked at Riley. "You remembered it, right?"

"Was I supposed to remember something?" Riley teased him.

Charlie went pale.

"I'm kidding. I have it in my bag," Riley promised.

"What do you have?" Ida asked.

"Carol's birthday present," Riley replied. "Relax, Charlie."

"Yeah, right—right. Yeah."

Andi laughed. "Do you need to practice?"

"Practice?" Ida was confused. "What does he need to practice?"

Charlie shifted his weight from foot to foot.

"What is going on?" Ida said. "I haven't finished one margarita so I know I'm not drunk or hallucinating. What are you all up to?"

"I just... I'm not sure how to start," Charlie said. "I mean, what do I say?"

Andi looked at Fallon. "Show him, Fallon."

"What?" Fallon asked.

"You and Riley. Show him," Andi said.

"Me and Riley?"

"Sure. You've made one and she's accepted one before."

"Not exactly," Riley said, understanding what Andi was suggesting.

Andi ignored the comment and continued. "Come on, Fallon," she goaded her lover. "I know there's a romantic hiding in there."

Why are you doing this, Andi? Fallon had an idea what was driving Andi's suggestion and it made her more than a little uncomfortable. Andi had been making comments for a few weeks subtly intimating that Fallon's feelings for Riley might be changing. Fallon refused to examine that possibility much less discuss it.

"Is someone going to tell me what the hell is going on?" Ida asked.

"Fallon will show you," Andi said.

Riley looked between Fallon and Andi. Andi's tone was playful. Fallon's expression was unreadable. Riley tried to surmise whether she saw anger or pain in Fallon's eyes. Perhaps it was a mixture of the two.

"Do you have it?" Fallon asked Riley, her gaze still locked with Andi's.

Riley reached in her bag and pulled out the box that held Carol's ring. Fallon accepted it and took Riley's hand, leading her a few feet away.

"Pay attention, Charlie," Fallon said. "This is something you hopefully only do once."

"Fallon," Riley pulled Fallon down and whispered in her ear. "You don't have to do this."

Fallon took a step back. She looked at Riley and smiled. *Okay, Andi.* Riley's concerned gaze touched Fallon. Then again, everything about Riley Main seemed to touch Fallon. *Goddamn you, Andi.* She took a deep breath. Riley smiled at her and her heart immediately sped up without warning. *Oh, no. No. Shit.* Two more deep breaths and Fallon began to speak.

"I'm not particularly good with words," Fallon said. She took another breath.

Andi watched, the truth she'd suspected tugging her heart. Fallon wasn't ready to face her reality. In truth, neither was Andi. No one could outrun the truth. And, Riley? Andi was positive that Riley hadn't begun to explore her feelings for Fallon. That much Andi did know. She also was sure those feelings existed. It was written across both their faces. A gentle nudge was in order. It hurt like hell to give it. She needed to. Both Riley and Fallon were reluctant to let go, to allow themselves to take a risk with their hearts. Loss could do that to a person. It was the guilt brought on by that loss that held Riley and Fallon back; Riley fearing she might somehow betray her husband despite the reality that he was gone, and Fallon? Fallon continued to see the failure of her relationship with Olivia as her fault. She sang a different story when she discussed their parting, but Andi was aware that deep down Fallon blamed herself. If love was God's greatest gift; guilt was the devil's greatest weapon.

Guilt led to fear and doubt. Fear and doubt prevented a person from living fully.

Riley held her breath. *This isn't real.* It wasn't real. It was make-believe. Why did her chest suddenly ache with anticipation? No one had ever looked at her the way Fallon was right now. Or maybe it was that she'd never felt quite the way she did looking at Fallon. *I'm losing my mind.*

Ida glimpsed Andi's expression from the corner of her eyes. *Oh, Andi.*

Fallon's brain seemed incapable of making her mouth work. She closed her eyes for a second. *What the hell is wrong with me?* Riley's hand found hers and Fallon's eyes opened. Riley's smile banished thought. Suddenly, Fallon found her voice. "If I've learned anything in my life it's that you never know what the next moment is going to bring. I don't know what's going to happen tomorrow. I do know that I want you to be part of it—tomorrow and the next day and the next day after that."

Riley's hand trembled as it held Fallon's. *Why am I shaking?*

"Every day," Fallon said. She let go of Riley's hand and opened the box. "Will you? Marry me?"

Riley stared at Fallon. Why did she feel like crying? Would anyone ever want that from her again? Would she be able to give it to anyone? *Fallon.* Would Fallon ever want to share that with anyone? With her? *Riley, snap out of it!*

"Umm, Riley?"

Riley snapped to attention. "Yes," she whispered. *Someday I want to share that—someday.*

Fallon slipped Carol's ring onto Riley's finger and pulled her close.

Riley's breath caught.

Andi bit the inside of her lip.

Fallon searched Riley's eyes for a moment. *Riley.* She caught herself and took a step back. "And then you kiss the girl," she said. She turned to Charlie.

Charlie's chin nearly touched the floor. "Wow. Wow," he said. "That's… Wow. She said yes, Fallon."

Riley chuckled. She took the ring off her finger, placed it in the box, and handed it to Charlie. "And so will Carol."

"Yeah." He looked at Fallon. "Could you write that down for me?"

Fallon rolled her eyes. "Come on, I'll walk you out."

Riley steadied her breathing. "I'm going to go call Marge and check on Owen," she said.

Ida turned to look at Andi. "Why did you do that?"

Andi's eyes glistened with sadness. Underneath it Ida saw something else—love.

"Because I love them both," Andi said.

Ida nodded. "I do too. She does love you, Andi."

Andi smiled. "She deserves more than I can give her."

"And, Riley? You know, Riley has had…"

"If I had to place a bet, I would bet that Riley accepts it before Fallon." Her eyes found Riley in the distance outside the door. "If I had a daughter…"

"Mmm." Ida followed Andi's gaze. She took Andi's hand and held it. "You deserve more too."

Andi smiled. *I'm not sure I know what more there is.*

CHAPTER NINE

"Hey!" Fallon called for everyone's attention. The dull roar of the crowded pub continued to hum.

"How does she expect to quiet them down?" Riley asked.

Ida stood up, put her thumb and forefinger to her lips and whistled.

"You could always do that," Riley commented.

Fallon shook her head. "Thank you, Mom."

Ida took a slight bow.

Riley laughed. "This whole town is nuts." She glanced at Andi and took hold of Andi's arm. "Hey, are you okay?" Riley asked.

Andi winked and pointed to Fallon. "Let's see if Fallon's proposal helped."

"Carol," Fallon said. "Charlie wanted this to be a special birthday for you so I will give him the floor. Charlie…"

Charlie stepped up and looked at Carol.

Carol's smile was infectious. That's what Riley thought. It had been a lively party so far. Riley guessed the crowd at about sixty people. Calling it close quarters would've been an understatement. Riley scanned the crowd. Charlie was a nervous wreck. Fallon looked amused. Pete and Dale looked confused—a permanent state of being from Riley's perspective. Ida appeared to be slightly inebriated and ready to whoop with excitement at any second, that or fall over. And, Andi, Andi was quiet. Riley couldn't recall a time when Andi had remained silent for more than a few minutes. She was smiling, but Riley detected sorrow in her friend. *What's that about, I wonder?* She loved Andi. She'd told Andi more about her feelings than she had anyone. Andi was open with her about nearly everything. Andi was also protective. Perhaps Andi felt their sisterhood similarly. *I wish you'd talk to me.*

"Stop worrying about me," Andi whispered. "Listen." She gestured to Charlie.

Charlie stuttered. "I… Well, I… I know it's your birthday and you're not supposed to combine things or whatever. I heard that I think. You know, like you shouldn't do it on Christmas or Valentine's Day or whatever, but I know that your birthday hasn't always been the best day so I thought… You know…"

"Charlie!" Carol called for her boyfriend's attention.

Charlie froze.

Carol shook her head. "What are you talking about?"

Charlie sucked in a long breath and dropped to his knee.

Carol's hand covered her mouth.

"I'm not as romantic as Fallon. She has this thing down."

Fallon shook her head.

Riley laughed. *She certainly does.*

Carol looked at Fallon curiously.

"Don't ask," Fallon said.

Charlie took another deep breath. "Anyway. I want this day to be special from now on—a day you can look forward to. I don't know what I did to get so lucky," he said. "I love you. I mean, I really love you. I want all those things we've talked about. You know, kids and a house of our own with a front porch swing. So… I… Will you marry me, Carol?"

A few tears slipped over Carol's cheeks. "You know I will."

Charlie let out relieved breath. His hand trembled as he took the ring from the box and slipped it on Carol's finger.

Carol giggled. "Are you going to stand up and kiss me?"

"Oh." Charlie found his feet. He pulled her close and kissed her softly.

"That was perfect," Ida called out her approval. Thunderous clapping and whoops of congratulations erupted.

Andi finished the last sip of her margarita. "On that note."

"Andi." Riley caught her friend by the arm.

Andi smiled. "I told you to stop worrying about me."

"Are you okay to drive?"

"I think I'm going to take a walk first," Andi said. "I'll see you later."

Riley's forehead crinkled with concern. She watched as Ida gently squeezed Andi's hand as Andi left.

Ida found her way back to the bar and picked up her margarita. "She'll be okay."

"I wish she'd talk to me."

"Mm. She cares about you, Riley."

Riley's heart dropped. *Something is wrong.* "I tell her everything."

"I know you do. You look up to her."

"More like I trust her."

"With good reason," Ida offered.

Riley's voice dropped to almost a whisper. "She's like the big sister I always wanted."

Ida patted Riley's hand. *And, you are the daughter she's always wished she had.* "Come on, I'll buy you a free drink."

Riley nodded.

"Where's Andi?" Fallon asked when she reached the bar.

"She had some things she needed to take care of," Ida said.

Fallon was about to question her mother. Ida's gaze told her to let the subject drop. *Guess I'll have to wait to find out what that's about.* Jake was due early the next morning. She would have to wait a week to talk to Andi freely.

"Oh, my God, Fallon." Carol came up behind the group and spun Fallon to face her. "Thank you for everything." She looked at Riley. "And, thank you."

"I didn't do anything," Riley said.

"Charlie said you helped him with the ring."

"Nothing more than moral support," Riley assured her.

"Anyway, thank you," Carol said. She hugged Riley and then Fallon. "It's the best day of my life," she said before being pulled away.

"I'm happy for them," Riley said. "Ida's right; it was perfect."

"Oh?" Fallon began. "More perfect than mine?"

"Yours?"

"Yeah, my proposal."

Riley smiled. "Some woman is going to count herself lucky one day." She kissed Fallon on the cheek and hopped off the barstool.

Fallon watched as several people stopped Riley on her way to the jukebox. When she turned back around, Ida handed Fallon a beer. "What's that look for?"

"What look?" Ida asked.

"That one."

"I have no idea what you're talking about."

"Right. How much of my tequila have you consumed?"

"Not enough to get me to tell you what you want me to."

"Which is?" Fallon asked.

"What you need to hear but won't listen to."

Fallon rolled her eyes. "Has anyone paid for a drink today?"

Ida shrugged. "You said to keep the tab open."

"Charlie's tab, Mom."

Ida shrugged again.

"I don't know how I ever make money in this place with you around."

"Drink your beer."

Fallon took a sip. Her eyes drifted to Riley. *Now, what is going on there?*

"Hey, Riley."

"Hi, Jerry. How are you?"

"Good. Good. Pretty good. You?"

Riley smiled. "I can't complain."

"Where's your little guy?"

"Oh, Marge offered to watch him," Riley explained.

"Ah… So…"

Riley raised her eyebrow.

"I was kind of wondering if maybe you might like to have dinner sometime… With me, I mean."

Riley forced herself not to laugh. She wouldn't have imagined that Jerry Walker would be nervous to ask anyone on a date. She doubted that many women would refuse. Jerry was about 6'1 with sandy-brown hair and hazel eyes. She could easily imagine him donning a page in a construction worker's calendar. He possessed rugged good looks, completely different from Robert. Robert had been handsome, but slight in his build. *Funny.* Robert had bordered on cocky when he first approached Riley. Jerry was stumbling. *Never judge a book by its cover.*

"Jerry, are you asking me out on a date?"

Jerry blushed. "Well… I mean, it's dinner with me so… But, I mean if you want to bring Owen…"

"I'd love to," Riley said. *You have to start somewhere.*

"Really?"

Riley chuckled. "You still have my number?"

He nodded.

"You let me know when," Riley said. She offered him a smile and headed off to dance with Carol.

Fallon sighed.

Ida's lips tightened thoughtfully. "She's quite the catch."

"What?"

"Riley," Ida said. "She's quite the catch."

Fallon's stomach flipped violently. "Yeah."

Ida shook her head. *Sometimes, Fallon, I could just smack you.*

May 15th

"What are you doing?" Carol laughed. Fallon was putting the finishing touches on what appeared to be a birthday present. The two packages were wrapped in a watercolor print paper with purple bows. "It's a kid's party. A little boy's party with a car theme. What is that?"

Fallon felt her face flush. She'd found out purely by accident that Riley's birthday was the week after Owen's. For some reason, Riley hadn't shared that with anyone. Fallon wasn't certain why. She'd asked Andi if there was some reason that Riley would want to keep her birthday a secret.

Fallon finished tying her shoes and leaned over to kiss Andi. "Everything okay with you?"

Andi smiled. "Not you too."

"Me too?"

"You and Riley. Stop worrying about me."

"That's not going to happen," Fallon said. "Ever."

"I'm fine. I'd be better if you climbed back in this bed."

Fallon grinned. "Yeah, so would I."

"Duty calls?" Andi guessed.

"Carol and Charlie are visiting her mother in New York tomorrow. I told her to take tonight off. They already set a date for the wedding."

"I'm not surprised."

Fallon groaned.

"What is it?" Andi wondered.

"Did Riley mention anything about her birthday?"

"Her birthday? No. Why?"

"She tells you everything, Andi."

"She hasn't said a word."

"Weird."

"Why is that weird?" Andi wondered.

"Her birthday is the week after Owen's."

"Really?"

"Yeah."

"She didn't mention anything to me."

"She didn't to me either," Fallon said.

"Fallon, don't make something out of nothing. She might just be so busy concentrating on Owen's birthday that she didn't think about it."

Fallon stared at Andi.

"Okay, I'll admit it's a little strange. If there is a reason she hasn't told us, it's hers to tell when she's ready," Andi said.

Fallon sighed.

"What?" Andi asked.

"Do you remember when Charlie proposed?"

"How could I forget?"

"Yeah, but do you remember that he said Carol didn't always have a happy birthday?"

"I seem to recall that; yes."

"What if that's it? What if the reason she hasn't said anything is that she has some bad memory of that day?"

Andi smiled at Fallon. Fallon was falling in love. Andi had known it for a while. Every day she seemed to find more evidence glaring at her. If she dared suggest the possibility to Fallon, she would be met with forceful denials; denials that would likely push Fallon to bury her feelings deeper. Part of Andi was tempted to do that. It would benefit her, wouldn't it? No. It wouldn't. She loved Fallon. She loved Riley. Andi guessed that she understood Riley better than most people. It was odd, even to her. She'd always thought that if Fallon met someone, she would harbor some amount of resentment. She did feel a modicum of jealousy. Resentment? Not a drop. Andi could see the wheels turning in Fallon's head. The fact that Riley might hold back from Fallon didn't surprise her. Riley was falling too—hard. Where Fallon sought to suppress, ignore, or deny her feelings, Riley had yet to examine them at all. That was one of the reasons that Riley shared facts and tidbits, engaged in banter and flirtation with Fallon but chose to confide her fears and feelings to Andi. Riley loved Andi. Riley was falling in love with Fallon, and while it was not con-

scious, something within Riley kept pressing the brakes. Whatever Riley's reason for not sharing her upcoming birthday, Andi thought it wise to tread lightly.

"If you want my advice, don't make a big deal about it," Andi said.

"You don't think we should say something?"

"We? I'm not pressing this with Riley. When she's ready to talk, if there is anything that she needs to talk about, she will let one or both of us know."

Fallon grumbled.

"If you really feel that you should say something do it gently. Don't ask her what the issue is, Fallon. Just mention that you know. How do you know?"

"She left her license out on the table the other night. She was looking all over for it. I noticed it when I handed it to her."

Andi nodded. "Do what feels right," she said.

"I don't know what feels right," Fallon replied.

"Yes, you do," Andi disagreed.

"Are we still talking about Riley's birthday?"

Andi smiled. "Just do what your heart tells you to do."

Fallon shook her head. She leaned in and kissed Andi.

"What was that for?" Andi asked.

"Just doing what my heart told me."

Andi sighed. Fallon was not going to make life easy. She placed a sweet kiss on Fallon's lips. "I'll see you later."

"Pastels, Fallon? For a three-year-old boy?" Carol asked. "What did you get him; *The Guide to Bartending?*" Carol teased.

"Very funny. For your information, I got Owen something special. This is for a friend."

"Something special, huh? You bought him skis, didn't you?"

Fallon smiled.

"You did!"

"Maybe. I got him something he can play with now too."

"How much did you buy him?" Carol asked.

"Why does it matter?"

"I count on you for my paycheck. If Riley kills you, I'm broke."

"She won't kill me."

"Uh-huh."

Fallon laughed. "Don't be so dramatic."

"Please tell me that whatever you got won't involve dirt."

"What are you talking about? Have you been hitting the vodka?"

"No. You tortured poor Riley that whole month she did your laundry."

"I don't know what you're talking about."

Carol crossed her arms. "Really? Sledding in the mud with Owen? Ring any bells?"

"Sledding in the *snow*. I can't help that there is mud *under* the snow," Fallon said.

"Uh-huh. Making pizza with Owen? Does that ring any bells?"

"He likes to help in the kitchen."

"I'm sure. How about this one; painting your spare room with Owen. Because everyone asks a two-year-old to help with that."

Fallon chuckled. "I think she threw that outfit out."

"See? She had to throw out Owen's clothes because of you."

"Not Owen's," Fallon replied.

"Oh, my God. You are *never* babysitting my kids… When I have them."

Fallon shrugged.

"So? What else did you get him?"

"None of your business. I don't trust you not to tell Riley anyway. What did *you* get him?"

Carol smirked. "Charlie and I got him a talking dinosaur."

Fallon laughed. *And, you're worried about Riley being mad at me for dirt?*

"Why are you laughing? Owen loves dinosaurs."

"I know. That doesn't mean Riley does."

"Why wouldn't Riley like dinosaurs? It's cute."

"I'm sure it is." Fallon grabbed her presents and headed for the backroom of the pub. Noisy toys definitely beat messy toys on the annoyance scale. She had removed the batteries from more than one of Evan, Emily, and Summer's toys over the years. Carol had a lot to learn.

"Hey, Fallon?" Carol poked her head around the corner.

"Yeah?"

"Your mom just pulled in the lot."

"At two in the afternoon?"

Carol shrugged.

I wonder what that's about. Fallon made her way to the front door. "Mom?"

Ida stepped out of her car and looked over her shoulder. "Expecting someone else?"

"I wasn't expecting anyone. Are you okay?"

"Of course, I'm okay."

"What are you doing here?"

"It's nice to see you too, dear."

"You know what I mean."

Ida grinned. "I need to talk to you."

"Okay?"

"Let's go inside."

Fallon held the door open for her mother. "Does this conversation require me to pour alcohol?"

Ida's wan smile answered the question.

"Margarita?" Fallon asked.

"Maybe after."

"What's going on?"

Ida sat down at a table and directed Fallon to sit across from her.

"Seriously, what's going on?"

"I need to leave on Sunday," Ida said.

"Leave? Where are you going?"

"Your brother called."

"Okay?"

Ida sighed heavily. "He's being sent overseas."

"Where?" Fallon asked.

"He couldn't say."

"How long?"

"Couldn't say that either."

Fallon attempted to process her mother's news. Dean had entered the Naval Academy after high school. He had worked in Naval Intelligence for years. She wasn't sure what *exactly* Dean did now. He'd been stationed in Virginia, Japan, Kuwait, Hawaii and for longer than Fallon thought was usual, Dean had been working in Washington DC. She had thought that Dean's next piece of news would regard his retirement. An overseas trip or deployment was the last thing she anticipated. She was sure that her mother felt the same way.

"So… You're going down to see him before he leaves."

"I am. I plan to stay for a few weeks."

"A few weeks?" Fallon questioned.

"Until Evan gets out of school."

"Mom, that's a month."

"Well, four weeks."

"A month."

Ida shrugged.

"Why? Evan is almost thirteen. Why would you need to be there? Beth should be able to handle it for a few weeks. I mean, Mom, she's handled it for years."

Ida sighed.

"What am I missing?"

"I just found out myself."

Fallon was growing both concerned and irritated. "Found out what?"

"Beth's pregnant."

Fallon was stunned. Her sister-in-law was forty-two. If she had thought news of Dean being sent overseas was surprising, hearing that Beth was pregnant was mind-blowing.

"You look surprised," Ida commented.

"You're not?" Fallon challenged.

"I am," Ida confessed.

"I still don't get why you need to go there."

"Dean's concerned."

"Is there a reason to be?"

"I think I'll know more when I get there," Ida offered.

"What do you need me to do?" Fallon asked.

"Other than take care of yourself?"

"Other than that."

"That's not enough?"

Fallon laughed. "I'll be okay, Mom."

Ida sighed. Fallon would be *okay*. The tide in Fallon's life was shifting. Ida wasn't sure if Fallon recognized that as clearly as those closest to her did. She hated leaving now for any length of time. She worried; worried far more about her daughter than she ever had her son, and not for the reasons she knew Fallon would suggest. Dean had always excelled at whatever he sought to try. Fallon had spent more energy than Ida could understand trying to compete with or surpass her brother. It didn't matter if it was on a ski slope, in a classroom, or financially. Part of it was Fallon's admiration of Dean. Part of it was some crazy notion Fallon had developed that Dean's success somehow mitigated hers. Despite Fallon's need to compete with her older brother, the two had always maintained a close relationship. In recent years, Fallon had distanced herself from him. The truth was Dean's decision to help Olivia and Barb have a family had hurt Fallon deeply. It was the one time that Ida saw resentment in her daughter's eyes—betrayal. Ida couldn't blame Fallon. She loved both her children. She'd always liked Olivia, and she adored all her grandchildren. Losing Olivia had torn Fallon apart. Watching Olivia start the family they had planned with someone else would have been painful on its own. Knowing that Dean had agreed to help in that endeavor shattered Fallon's trust. Fallon closed herself off more than Ida had ever thought possible. For the first time in many years, Ida watched as Fallon's resolve slowly began to crack. Fallon had two people she let close; two people she cared for immensely—Andi and Riley. She would not be able to keep Andi if she hoped to pursue a relationship with Riley. It was a precarious time, not a time that Ida would choose to be distant from her daughter.

"Seriously, Mom, I'll be fine."

Ida nodded. "Do me a favor."

"Anything."

"Don't bury yourself in this place while I'm gone."

What was it with everyone lately? Andi had made similar comments. Riley was constantly suggesting that Fallon needed to step out of the pub more. Even Carol had taken to urging Fallon to take time off. Fallon offered her mother a strained smile. "I promise."

Ida shook her head. "No matter what happens, Fallon; don't lock yourself up in here."

"Mom, it's Whiskey Springs. What is going to happen? The only earth shattering thing that might happen one day is Pete having sex."

Ida couldn't stop herself from chuckling. She sobered quickly. "I'm serious."

"I promise; I won't let *Murphy's Law* be my life."

I hope not, Fallon. I hope not.

CHAPTER TEN

"I'm glad that you wanted to get together," Riley said.

"I thought you could use a little adult time," Andi commented.

"You thought right."

"How was your *date* with Jerry?" Andi wondered.

Riley shrugged. She liked Jerry. He had been so nervous for the first hour they spent together that she had been forced to carry their conversation. Eventually, he had relaxed enough to engage. They talked mainly about work; how he started his business and what had led Riley to take up editing. She enjoyed getting to know him. He seemed genuinely interested in what she shared. Riley didn't talk much about her work with friends. The exception being Fallon. For some reason, Fallon seemed to find Riley's work fascinating. That had surprised her. It wasn't glamorous, and she didn't believe most people would find the ins and outs of her days terribly interesting. Still, she loved it. She also hoped that it would serve her as a writer one day. That was her ultimate dream; to write at least one memorable novel. She'd tried to start a thousand times and never seemed to get past a few paragraphs. Riley had chalked up her failure to keep moving with a project to time constraints. Working from home had been a Godsend as a single mother. When she did finish with the work that paid her bills, she wanted to devote her time to Owen. Since arriving in Whiskey Springs, she'd found herself inclined to spend her free-time investing in new friendships, Fallon and Andi's most of all.

While a lack of time contributed to Riley's lack of productivity on the writing front, she knew that something deeper was blocking her. Perhaps she wasn't ready to be vulnerable, to explore the emotions that writing a story would demand. Talking with Jerry had prompted her to examine her future.

"It was fine," Riley said.

"Fine?" Andi chuckled. "A few weeks ago, you were ready to throw Pete against a wall. Was Jerry that boring?"

Riley laughed. "No. Actually, our conversation got me thinking about some things."

"What things?"

"What do I want to do? With my career, I mean."

"Your career?"

"I know. I didn't leave wondering when I'd see him again. I spent that night thinking about work. I guess our dinner didn't exactly ignite that romantic spark I'd hoped."

Not surprised. "It happens."

"I'm not sure what will do that."

"I don't know. I think sparks fly when you least expect them to."

"Like you and Fallon?"

Andi smiled. *Like me and Fallon.* "That would be an example."

"How did you…"

"How did we end up sleeping together?"

"It's none of my business."

"Do you really want to know?" Andi asked. *Do you, Riley?*

Riley felt a lump form in her throat. *Why do I want to know?* It was a logical question to ask. Riley was curious. "I'm curious," she admitted.

Andi nodded. "Fallon and I have been friends for years."

"I know."

"I think she had a crush on me when she was a kid." Andi chuckled. *I know she did.* "Back then she was a kid."

It was easy for Riley to imagine Fallon as a kid. She guessed that Fallon had never seen herself that way, though.

"When she moved back," Andi continued. "We started to get to know each other in a different way. The boys were young. She actually taught Jacob to ski. He struggled. Everything athletic came naturally to Dave. It was harder for Jacob. Being older, I think he felt he should be leading all the time. Jake was hardly ever home even back then. He didn't have time to take the boys skiing or fishing; not often anyway. Not that he doesn't love them; he's always been on the go. Fallon and I had a standing lunch on Wednesday's. Most of the time it was at the pub, which I have to tell you was a complete dump back then." Andi laughed. "Sometimes, I still can't believe she managed to put that place back together. She won't quit once she gets her mind set on something."

"I've noticed."

"Mm. Well, that day Jacob had a mini-meltdown. He and Dave had gone with their uncle for a day at the slopes. Jacob was about six. Dave was only four. Their uncle dropped them off at the pub to me. Apparently, Dave had coasted as if he'd been on skis his whole life. Jacob spent most of the day face-down in the snow."

"Oh no."

"Yep. He was so sullen. When I asked him what had happened, he erupted into tears. Fallon put all the pieces together. I'll never forget that day. She pulled him onto her lap and promised to teach him. She did. She took him the next day, just him. Spent hours skiing backwards until he found his feet. Whenever she would decide to spend a day at the slopes, she'd invite the kids, and she never let Jacob quit. That was a long, long time ago. I think Fallon captured a little piece of my heart that day."

Fallon loved kids. As a parent, watching someone connect with your child touched you. Riley loved to watch Fallon with Owen. "I understand."

Andi smiled. *I know you do.* "She and Jacob became close. I think that she's his hero; if you want to know the truth."

Fallon often talked about Andi's older son. Riley knew that she had spent time with Andi's kids over the years. Fallon's affection for them wasn't news. She'd listened to countless stories about Jacob and Dave from both Fallon and Andi. It wasn't news that the two women had been close friends for years either. Riley wondered how a friendship that had been cultivated over many years led to an affair.

Andi continued. "When Dave was getting ready to leave for college last summer, I struggled. Both Jacob and Dave would be gone. Jacob got a great offer. He was working as an intern in Boston for the summer. His father was away for six weeks. Jake had invited Dave to travel with him to London and Paris. I was home alone. I think Jacob worries about me." She chuckled. "Jacob called and asked if I thought Fallon would come with me for a weekend to Boston. He wanted to show us what he was working on."

"Fallon mentioned that he was a talented artist."

Andi beamed. "I know I'm not impartial, but that's an understatement. He was working on an ad campaign for Toyota. That doesn't happen for twenty-year-olds often."

"I wouldn't imagine so."

"He was so excited. I swear to you, everything he does, he wants to show Fallon."

"Fallon talks about him often." That was true. She talked about Jacob Maguire at least as much as she did her goddaughters or Evan.

"Anyway…. I didn't think she'd go. You know her. She likes to stick close to home."

"But she agreed."

"She did. It was one of the best weekends of my life," Andi said. She sighed lightly. There was no point in avoiding this conversation. Sooner or later Riley was going to ask, and eventually either she or Fallon would need to tell the young woman how they had ended up in the strange relationship they shared. Andi had been thinking about that weekend often, and she knew the reason why. She would forever recall that weekend as one of the most memorable and special times in her life. She would spare Riley the details, although she would never be able to recall that weekend without reliving it vividly.

Jacob had brought Andi and Fallon into a large conference room. Easels surrounded a long table. He'd taken them through the campaign, pointing out the graphic work he'd done and the notes that credited him. He glowed. It made Andi's heart sing. Afterward, Fallon had insisted on taking them all to a celebratory dinner. Jacob had gotten an offer to join some of his coworkers at a party. He'd been ready to decline. Fallon wouldn't hear of it. "Leave us old ladies to our drinks," she had told him. Andi remembered the grateful hug that Jacob bestowed on them both, more like the affection she would expect from a child Owen's age than a young man working in the city.

Fallon had suggested they continue their evening at the hotel bar. With no place to be, and no need to drive they had indulged in a few drinks. When Fallon walked Andi to her room, Andi had become emotional. Andi still wasn't certain what had prompted her tears; whether it was the reality that her children were becoming adults, that she would be alone at home soon, or the way Fallon looked at her. Maybe it was a little bit of everything. She could still feel the heat of Fallon's hand as it pressed to her cheek. No matter how many times Andi replayed their first kiss, she could never determine who had initiated it. It didn't matter. Fallon's lips had found hers. Her hands had gripped Fallon's waist, and everything in the world had faded away. It had been the one and only night that she had slept in Fallon's arms. They'd agreed the next day that they would never regret that night but would never repeat it. That agreement had been broken two days later. It was that night, the second time that she and Fallon had fallen into each other's arms that they had agreed never to spend an entire night together again. Andi had no intention of leaving Jake. Fallon had no desire to break up Andi's marriage. Neither wanted to think about walking away from what they had discovered. For nearly a year, they had come together whenever possible. Andi would never regret her time with Fallon. Recently, she had come to face realities that she had chosen to deny. What she felt for Fallon, what she shared with Fallon went far beyond a sexual affair. She chose not to name what she felt. Maybe that would make the inevitability of an ending more bearable—maybe.

Riley listened as Andi fell into her memories. Emotions flickered in Andi's eyes like fireworks—attraction, lust, affection, joy, sadness, and there is was—love. She took Andi's hand without comment.

"Fallon is one of a kind," Andi told Riley.

So are you. "Can I ask you something?"

Andi nodded.

"Why didn't you two want to try? Being together."

Andi smiled. There were many reasons. "I'm not sure I can answer that. A lot of reasons, I suppose. I'm not sure that we would work as a couple."

Riley decided not to offer her assessment that they were a couple, albeit in a difficult situation.

Andi read her friend's thoughts and shook her head. "No," she said. "We aren't a couple, Riley. We're lovers. It's not the same. I'm not saying that I don't feel something for Fallon. That would be a lie. Our relationship doesn't come with all the expectations and responsibilities that being a couple does."

"Do you think that's why it sparked? Because you don't have to deal with all the other *stuff*?"

"No."

"But it did spark."

"Like a lightning storm," Andi said.

"Yeah, that didn't happen with Jerry. Maybe I'm broken."

Or maybe he's just not the one to ignite that flame. "I don't think so. Are you going to see him again?"

Riley shrugged. "You and Fallon were friends for years before you felt something. A few more dinners couldn't hurt."

Andi nodded. *I wish that were true, Riley.* "So, enough about my twisted love life. What about this party?"

❧   ❧   ❧

Fallon sat at the kitchen table stuffing party bags. Riley had been observing Fallon with interest all night. Something was off with her friend. Riley wasn't sure how to approach the subject.

"Thanks for helping," Riley said.

"I think I should be thanking you."

"What are you talking about? You're letting me have Owen's party at your house. You're spending a Friday night putting party favors in bags. I'm sure there are things you'd rather be doing." Fallon's halfhearted smiled tugged at Riley's heart.

"Not really. Besides, you've done two loads of laundry since you've been here."

"Ah, the real reason you suggested the party move to your house."

Fallon chuckled. She was happy to offer her house to Riley. It was larger than Riley's and would accommodate Owen's playmates and Riley's friends regardless of the weather. Riley seeking out Fallon's laundry and sorting it was a bonus to be sure. Riley being at Fallon's was always a bonus.

"Fallon?"

"Hum?"

"Is there something bothering you?"

Fallon sighed.

"Everything okay with you and Andi?"

What is she talking about? "Why? Did Andi say something to make you think it isn't?"

"Not at all. You just seem a little *off* tonight."

"My mom is leaving Sunday for a month."

"Leaving? Where is she going?"

"Dean's being sent overseas."

"Oh..."

Fallon sighed again. "Apparently, my sister-in-law is pregnant. He doesn't want to leave her alone. Mom's going to stay until Evan's out of school."

"I know you'll miss her."

"I will."

Riley studied Fallon for a moment. "It's not just that, is it?"

Fallon took a deep breath. She'd been feeling incredibly emotional all day. Preparing for Owen's party seemed to heighten that.

"Fallon?"

"It's stupid."

"I doubt that."

"Okay, it's selfish."

Riley doubted that as well. "Care to share what's so stupid and selfish?"

Fallon hesitated. She didn't like talking about her feelings. Riley's eyes held concern—genuine concern. She could tell Riley anything. Riley would listen. Still, she hesitated. It was selfish and it was stupid as far as Fallon was concerned. She should be happy for Dean and Beth. She should've been happy for Olivia and Barb too. It wasn't that she didn't wish them well. There was a hole in Fallon's life, one that she wasn't sure anyone or anything would ever be able to fill. Sitting with Riley watching Owen run through her house while they prepared for his party reminded Fallon of that void. When Owen had grown tired, he'd sought out Fallon. She and Riley had tucked him into the lower bunk of the bedroom Fallon kept for her goddaughters; a bedroom that was quickly filling with more of Owen's toys than anything Emily, Summer or Evan would find interesting. She loved having Owen at the house. That wasn't the issue. The issue was that she hated seeing him leave.

When Fallon took any time to examine her feelings, she found them ludicrous. She enjoyed close relationships with both her goddaughters, with Evan, with Jacob, and now with Owen. Fallon was the "cool" aunt. She was the adult that had the luxury of spending fun time with the children in her life without having to play a significant role as a disciplinarian. Wasn't that the best of all worlds? Olivia often commented that Fallon got the best deal after their break-up. Dean had told his sister that she should count herself lucky not to have to endure daily diapers, colicky nights, defiant phases, and the stress that came with children finding their way. Those comments cut Fallon to the core. What did everyone think? Did everyone in her life think so little of her that they believed she would grow tired of a child? She placed some goodies in a bag, set it aside, and smiled.

"Fallon, you don't have to tell me anything."

"Sometimes, I guess I feel a little sorry for myself."

"I think we all do," Riley offered.

"Maybe. I know that I should be calling Dean to congratulate him on Beth's pregnancy."

"But?"

"I don't know. I will. It just… Sometimes, Riley I wonder what I did wrong."

Riley's brow furrowed. "Wrong?"

"When we sat down with the contractor to build this house, I thought we'd be having birthday parties here every year for years and years."

Riley understood. "If having Owen's party here is too much…"

"What? No," Fallon dismissed Riley's concern. "No. I want you to have it here." *I do*.

More than Fallon wanted to share, she was excited about Owen's party. Since Riley's arrival in town, Fallon had developed a bond with Owen. She saw him at least three times a week, and often saw him every day. When she didn't see him,

Riley would often call so that he could say goodnight. Fallon had fallen in love with the toddler. She looked at Riley and her heart suddenly lurched in her chest. Perhaps it wasn't just Owen who had captured her heart. *Don't go there, Fallon.*

Riley smiled gently at her friend. "You never know what might happen," she said. Fallon's eyes seemed to implore her for something. What was it? Was it hope? She reached across the table and took Fallon's hand. "Who's to say this house won't have toddlers running amok one day."

Fallon's stomach fluttered at Riley's touch. Something else happened when she met Riley's gaze; her spirits lightened measurably. "Yeah, tomorrow," Fallon replied cheekily.

"That's not what I meant."

"I'm not sure about that, Riley."

Riley wasn't sure what to say. Her conversation with Andi that afternoon came to mind. She'd often thought Fallon was the Pied Piper in disguise. The truth was that Fallon loved children. Fallon loved people. It was also obvious that Fallon had been hurt. For Fallon, that pain equated to lost trust. Riley was beginning to realize that it wasn't only trust in others that Fallon struggled with; it was trusting herself—trusting the future held possibility for her. It pained Riley. Fallon would make an amazing partner for someone. She was sensitive and caring, honest, intelligent, and most importantly, Fallon was devoted to the people she loved. It made her easy to love. Riley squeezed Fallon's hand. *You are easy to love.* It might be easy to love Fallon; Riley knew it would not be as simple to convince Fallon to invest in a relationship. The wound that Olivia's departure left was deep. It might have appeared to have healed, the scars it left were reluctance and doubt.

"Well," Riley began. "Tomorrow is unpredictable, Fallon. I need to believe that if it can be turned upside down by tragedy, it can be forever altered by something unexpected and wonderful. If that was your reality right now, we probably wouldn't be sitting here. I hope you don't mind if I selfishly enjoy the bene-fit of having you to do this with me."

"This?"

"Owen's party. I guess I haven't said it; I don't know if I would have the strength to do this without you. I know it wouldn't be as much fun." *That's the truth.*

Riley's words surprised Fallon. It made sense. In some way, Owen's birthday had to remind Riley of Robert. "I know there's no substitute for Robert being here."

Riley smiled. The next two weeks would be difficult for her. It wasn't just the memory of Robert standing beside her when Owen was born. It wasn't only the way that image conjured a renewed sense of loss, of what Robert would miss—of what she missed. It reminded her that Owen would never know the man who gave him life, and that hurt Riley more than anything else. Owen's birthday had fallen a week before hers. Riley's birthday was also the day she had married Robert. So many beginnings to celebrate, and they all seemed hell bent on sum-moning feelings of loss. Fallon's presence eased Riley's sadness. All the loss had led Riley here, here to Whiskey Springs and to people she had grown to love more than she could fathom in a short time.

"No," Riley said. "There's no substitute."

Fallon tried to smile.

"There's something new," Riley said. Voicing that truth nearly took her breath away. There was something new. She was looking forward to the next day, largely because Fallon would be part of it.

Fallon held her breath. Silence hovered. Riley's hand was still holding hers. Unconsciously, Riley's thumb had begun to caress Fallon's palm. Riley's touch aroused something far more potent than lust. Fallon didn't want to break the spell between them. *Fallon, stop.* She forced herself to take a breath and let it out slowly. "How about we cap the evening with an adult bev-erage and an adult movie?"

Riley arched an amused brow.

"That did not come out the way I meant it."

"Fallon, are you blushing?" Riley teased.

"No, I probably need to turn down the heat."

Riley struggled to keep her laughter in check. *You are adorable sometimes.* "So, what are you saying? You don't want to watch an *adult* movie with *me*?"

Fallon's cheeks flushed a deeper shade of crimson.

Riley grinned. Few things made her happier than being with Fallon. Behind Fallon's bravado existed the silliest, most sensitive person Riley had ever encountered. No one could ask for a better friend. Based on the way Andi's eyes glistened whenever Fallon was in the room or her name was raised, and the fact that Olivia seemed to know where Fallon was at every moment when she visited; Riley guessed that Fallon was an equally incredible lover. That thought made her heart beat slightly faster. *Jesus, Riley, you really need to do something about this frustration. You're wondering about Fallon? What is wrong with you?* The next thought she had made her giggle. *At least, you weren't thinking about Pete again.*

"What are you giggling about?" Fallon asked. "If you really want to watch a grown-up movie, I can make that happen."

Riley shrugged. "What; do you own some perverted version of *Friends* I've never heard of?"

"I wish," Fallon said.

Riley fell into a fit of laughter.

"That was out loud, wasn't it?" Fallon grimaced.

"Tell you what, you pick the movie. I'm happy to take perverted over *Super Why*. I'll make some popcorn."

"What's wrong with *Super Why*?"

"You're serious."

Fallon shrugged. "Owen loves it."

Mm-hum. Owen loves it because you watch it with him. "Well, you can watch it with Owen before his party."

"Speaking of that."

"Yeah?"

"Why don't you just crash here?"

"Fallon, I don't have anything here."

"Owen's out like a light. You have to be back here around eleven anyway. Run home and get what you need."

Riley stared at Fallon with disbelief.

"What? It's only nine. It'll take you half an hour at most."

Riley wondered what was driving Fallon's request. *It doesn't matter.* Fallon didn't need to explain anything. Loneliness, that was the culprit and Riley and Owen were the cure. At least, they were for tonight. She smiled. "Okay."

Why was Fallon surprised? She had made the request.

Riley chuckled at the dumfounded look on Fallon's face. "Change your mind already?"

"What? No. I just…"

"Didn't expect me to agree?"

"I don't know," Fallon admitted.

"Is the offer still good?"

"The offer is always good." *Did I just say that?*

Riley smiled. "I'll keep that in mind." She kissed Fallon on the cheek. "I'm going to grab my jacket. I'll be back. How about you call Tony and order us a pizza? I'll pick it up on my way back."

"Are you hungry?" Fallon asked.

"Movies and pizza sound good to me, and one of your margaritas."

Fallon followed Riley to the front door. *What is it with the women in my life and margaritas?* "What do you want on the pizza?"

Riley shrugged and opened the door. "Surprise me."

"Be careful, Riley. You might not like it."

Riley winked. "I'm not worried." She closed the door.

Fallon's mouth went dry. *Jesus.* "Margaritas? I think I'll skip straight to the tequila."

CHAPTER ELEVEN

"Good Lord, is the whole town here?" Ida asked.

"She certainly meant it when she said she'd spread the word," Riley replied.

Ida shook her head. "I think she's having more fun than Owen."

Riley looked on affectionately. Fallon had purchased Owen a toddler basketball hoop. She had a group of children engaged in what could only have been deemed a ridiculous attempt at a basketball game. It might have looked absurd, six children with Fallon and Charlie making a pathetic attempt to instruct them. Laughter filled the air. Delighted squeals resulted in toddlers falling to the ground in fits of laughter. Riley wasn't sure who would need a nap more at the end of the party, Fallon or Owen. She laughed when Owen managed to grab the small ball. Fallon swooped in, picked him up and carried him to the hoop that stood at roughly his height.

"Slam dunk!" Fallon called out and spun Owen around.

"Fawon!" Owen laughed hysterically.

"She's certainly in her element," Andi commented.

Riley couldn't have wiped the stupid grin off her face if she tried, and she had no desire to try.

Andi watched as Fallon and Riley's eyes met. She felt Ida's hand press into her back. How they could deny it, avoid it or fail to see what was developing between them perplexed Andi.

Fallon's eyes drifted to Andi's and immediately expressed worry. Andi offered her a smile. Fallon's expression continued to convey her concern, and Andi forced herself to wink.

Ida wasn't sure whether her heart would burst with hope at seeing the way Fallon's eyes danced when they met Riley's or break from the sadness emanating from Andi. No matter how much living she did, Ida continued to be amazed at how love could be simple and complicated at the same time. Watching her children grow and her grandchildren thrive, losing the man she'd shared a lifetime with, all her living led Ida to the conclusion that the human heart was a well. It ran deep and it begged to be filled. Sometimes, a person could give so much that the well started to run dry. Other times it ran over, spilling out rivers that had nowhere to go. Love was like the rain. It poured down nurturing everything in its wake, filling the waiting well. Fallon's well had been depleted before she started her affair with Andi. Andi was the first sprinkle to fall into Fallon's heart in many years. Her presence had begun to refill the void that had left Fallon lonely. Riley? Riley was the looming storm. Ida thought that when the clouds broke, the well was sure to flow over, drowning the soft trickle that was Andi. Ida loved Andi Maguire like a daughter. She cherished her as a friend, and she was grateful to her as a mother.

"I hear there's some wine in the kitchen. Can I buy you a free drink?" Ida asked Andi.

"I'm game if you think we can find the tequila," Andi said. She squeezed Riley's shoulder and followed Ida to the kitchen.

Fallon managed to weave through a traffic jam of toddlers. She jogged over to Riley.

"Who won?" Riley asked.

"I don't know," Fallon confessed. "I lost track in the kerfuffle."

"Kerfuffle?"

"What? It's a word."

Riley smirked.

"It's in *Harry Potter*."

"Yes, it is." Riley's hand found Fallon's. "Thank you, Fallon."

"For what? The kerfuffle?"

"For everything."

Riley held Fallon's gaze steadily. Fallon's body tingled with the truth. *No, Fallon. You are seeing what you want to see. Let it go. It's Riley.*

Riley squeezed Fallon's hand. "I don't know what I'd do without you." She spoke the words so softly that Fallon had to strain to hear them.

"You don't ever have to find that out," Fallon promised.

Riley's eyes searched Fallon's. Emotions bubbled through her veins so quickly she couldn't think to name one. *I hope so.*

"Fawon!" Owen nearly tripped over his feet. "You help wif my twuck?"

Fallon beamed. Andi had purchased Owen a ride-on truck. Owen had tried it once before being lured away by Charlie to the basketball hoop. She flashed Riley a cheesy, hopeful grin.

"Go." Riley chuckled.

Fallon took Owen's hand and let him lead her away.

Riley unconsciously bit her lower lip. What would she do without Fallon?

❧ ❧ ❧

Ida grabbed Fallon by the arm. "Walk me to my car?"

"Sure."

"Fallon…"

"Yeah?"

Ida stopped and looked at her daughter.

"Mom? What is it?"

"You know, Andi cares about you."

Fallon was confused. Of course, she knew that Andi cared about her. She cared about Andi. "I care about her."

"I know you do."

"Mom, what is this about? Is Andi okay? You two disappeared for a while."

Ida wasn't sure how to answer. As much as Fallon liked to claim that Ida was opinionated about her children's lives; Ida never sought to interfere. She reveled in teasing Fallon. Denying that would be pointless. Everyone knew it. She wondered if Fallon realized how much ending her relationship with Andi would hurt them both. She adored Riley. Riley and Fallon were on a collision course with the emotions they held for the other. She also knew that pursuing a relationship with Riley would not be akin to a peaceful sunset sail. The overflowing well of feelings that would be unleashed was bound to create some murky landscapes to navigate. Falling in love with someone new didn't always mean you stopped loving the person you'd been holding. Ida and Andi had many long conversations. Andi understood that intimately. Ida feared that Fallon might underestimate the fallout of change, even if it was change for the best.

"Andi's okay," Ida said. "What about you?"

"Me? Why does everyone keep asking that?"

"Love is a wonderful thing, Fallon. Despite what people like to say it can hurt."

"I know," Fallon bit.

Ida sighed. "Yes, you do. We all get that lesson sooner or later. Be careful, Fallon."

Fallon wanted to argue. Andi was like a second daughter to Ida. It stood to reason that she would be worried about them both. Jake was due back in a few days. Dave and Jacob were both planning on coming home from school for the summer. All of it would complicate things for Andi and Fallon. Fallon sensed her mother was referencing something or rather, someone else. She had no intention of exploring that topic. "It's only a few weeks," Fallon said, "We'll all try not to break any hearts—at least until you're back."

Ida shook her head. "You're a pain in the ass."

"I know."

Ida embraced her daughter. "I love you, Fallon."

Fallon held onto her mother tightly. For some reason, she didn't want to let go. Ida was the one person on earth that Fallon could count on no matter what. That's what moms were for. She closed her eyes and thought about Andi and Jacob. Her thoughts drifted to Riley and Owen. *Yeah, that's what moms are for.* Fallon pulled away. "I love you too, Mom. Call me when you land, okay?"

"I will. Remember your promise."

"I made a promise?"

Ida rolled her eyes.

"I won't move into *Murphy's Law.*"

"Good."

Fallon watched her mother drive away. She sensed a presence behind her.

"You okay?" Riley gently took Fallon's arm.

"Yeah. I wish she wasn't going."

Riley made no comment. Instead, she took hold of Fallon's hand and led her back up the hill toward the house. "It's just Marge left at the house," she said. "She's cleaning up. It looks like Armageddon."

Fallon laughed. *Yeah, it probably does.*

"Silly string?" Riley shook her head.

"I have a shop-vac."

"Well, maybe we can just vacuum Owen too."

"Why?" Fallon stopped speaking when Owen started toward them on his truck. "Oh…"

"See what I mean?"

Owen was covered in silly string. He seemed delighted by his condition. "How did that happen?"

Riley shrugged. "I don't think I want to know."

"Mommy!" Owen called out. "Wook!"

"I see."

"I dwive! Fawon, I dwive!"

"How can he see to drive?" Fallon muttered.

Riley laughed. "You get the vacuum. I'll get Dale Earnhardt."

"It's a truck, Riley," Fallon said. She moved toward Owen. "Yeah?"

"Dale Earnhardt is a race car driver."

"So?"

Fallon spotted a can of silly string in a small compartment of Owen's truck. She grabbed it. "I'm going to get Mommy," she whispered in Owen's ear. She turned to face Riley, holding the can behind her back. "So?"

"Fallon, do you have a point?" Riley asked indignantly.

"Yeah, you need a lesson."

Riley blinked. "A lesson?"

Fallon's eyes twinkled with mischief. "Yep!" She charged Riley with the can.

"Fallon! No! Fallon!"

"Oh, yes, I think so."

Riley ran as fast as her feet could carry her. It wasn't fast enough. Fallon was on her heels in less than a second, spraying with abandon.

"Stop!" Riley laughed and grabbed for the can. Fallon tried to pivot away but Riley managed to get a grip on the can. The playful struggle sent them both to the ground, Fallon falling on top of Riley.

The laughter abruptly stopped when Riley's eyes met Fallon's. Fallon felt Riley beneath her, pressed against her. A gentle tug pulled at her heart. She wondered in that instant if anything existed between them—even air. It seemed there was no air to breathe. It had been siphoned away in Riley's presence, in her gaze. Fallon's eyes fell from soft pools of brown to the curve of Riley's lips. Riley was so close, closer than Fallon had ever dared to imagine. She lifted her gaze back to Riley's eyes. How long had they been here? Days? Hours? Moments? *Riley.*

A deep ache rose from within Riley, advancing like a wave before it tumbles ashore. It made sense. Fallon's eyes were so blue she was certain she could swim in them, drown in them. Had she ever seen anything so blue? They seemed to reflect the cresting wave rolling through Riley—blue, white, and stormy—*Fallon.*

"Mommy!" Owen's voice shattered the connection between them.

Riley's lips twitched deviously.

Fallon tilted her head. Without warning, a blast of silly string fell over her eyes.

"Ha!" Riley exclaimed triumphantly.

Owen laughed. "Fawon, Mommy gots you! Mommy gots you!"

"Oh, yeah?" Fallon rolled off Riley and grabbed hold of Owen. "Well, I've got you!"

"Fawon!" Owen giggled uncontrollably. "Mommy! Fawon gots me!"

Riley found her feet and watched as Fallon tossed silly string from the ground at Owen, letting him get a slight running start before pretending to struggle to catch him. The wave finally crested and crashed as happiness washed over her. *Fallon, what would I do without you.*

May 20th

Riley looked at the time on her phone. How long had she been talking to her sister? Too long. Only fifteen minutes? How was that possible? She flopped back onto the sofa and covered her eyes as Mary continued her diatribe.

"I don't understand why you insist on staying there," Mary said. "How are you ever going to meet someone in a town that has less people than where I work?"

Riley massaged her eyes. The last thing she wanted to deal with now was her sister's candid opinions about life—her life.

"Riley, are you there?"

"I'm here."

"Well? What is so appealing about living there? All your friends are here."

No, they aren't. "Not really."

"You've known these people a few months and suddenly they're more important than everyone who's stood by you all these years?"

"That's not what I'm saying, and you know it. I didn't come here for a vacation, Mary. I came here to try something new— to get a fresh start."

Mary groaned. "What about Owen?"

"Owen?"

"Yes, Owen—your son?"

Riley was reaching the limit of her patience. Owen was thriving in Whiskey Springs. Riley was still adjusting. Thriving would take time. It always did. "Owen loves it here. He has a playgroup with friends. He loved the snow." Riley giggled. *Probably because Fallon let him get so messy.* "He's happy, Mary."

"And, you?"

"It takes time."

"So, you're not happy."

"I didn't say that. I have friends too," she said.

"You have friends here."

"So, you have reminded me."

"What about that offer?"

"What offer?"

Mary sighed. "Derek Peters told me he reached out to you about a job."

Derek Peters was a friend of Riley's father, Doug. He'd worked for a major publisher for more than twenty years. He had reached out with an offer to Riley. The offer would entail her moving to either New York City or back to the West Coast. It also would mean that she would need to work in an office. She would have the opportunity to work with well-established and popular authors. It would help her make connections. She had considered it—seriously considered it. She didn't need the extra money. She could have taken a substantial amount of time off work had she cared to. Robert had left her enough money to support herself and Owen for a few years without working at all. She'd received a sizable settlement from the accident. Working was her choice. She needed to be self-sufficient. More than that, Riley loved her work. She didn't love her work more than she loved Owen. She had career aspirations. There was no role that Riley aspired to excel at more than being a mother. She was content and confident with her decision to work as a freelance editor from home.

"I'm not going to work for Derek," she told her sister.

"Riley, you can't be serious. All you've talked about since I can remember is writing a book. Derek can help you. Why would you pass this up?"

Riley's head was beginning to throb. *Why? Why? Why?* Mary's constant questioning reminded her of Owen's persistent, "Mommy. Mommy, Mommy." She chuckled. *Or Fawon, Fawon, Fawon.*

"Is something I said funny?" Mary's impatience was obvious.

"No." *No, it's annoying.* "I know you mean well…"

"I worry about you."

"I appreciate that. You don't need to. Honestly, things here are good."

"Good? Good or okay?"

"Good."

"At least tell me you still plan on visiting."

"I'll be there on the tenth just like we planned," Riley replied.

"What about your birthday?"

Riley sighed.

"What are you planning?"

"Nothing," Riley said.

"None of your *friends* are planning anything?" Mary asked. *Tread lightly, Mary.* "I don't think so."

"That's…"

"No one knows it's my birthday."

Mary was stunned. "I know it's a hard day, but…"

"It's just a day."

Oh, Riley, no it's not. "Why don't you come home sooner? Grab a flight."

"I'm all right," Riley promised. "Owen had a blast at his party. Everyone was here for that." *Everyone.*

Riley found herself smiling. She'd invited the families from Owen's playgroup, Andi, Ida, Carol and Charlie, and Marge. Fallon had "mentioned" the party to everyone she knew. It had taken an hour to get through opening Owen's presents. There had been games for the kids and loads of lively adult conversation. The day had ended with Owen asleep between Riley and Fallon on the sofa. Riley had glanced over to find Fallon had drifted off as well. She'd been content to sip her wine quietly until her glass was drained and her eyes fluttered and closed. She had a vague impression of Fallon covering her and Owen with a blanket. She didn't need to celebrate her birthday. Owen's party had turned into a two-day event. The next morning, they had shared breakfast, piled Owen's presents in Fallon's truck, and headed to Riley's. Day turned to evening, and Riley found herself making dinner for them. Fallon finally left when Owen fell asleep. It was the best present anyone could have given her.

"You should do something for your birthday."

Please, let this go. "I'll be happy with a nice bottle of wine and a good book," Riley said. "Listen, I should go. I need to feed Owen."

"Call me if you need anything," Mary said.

Riley knew the offer was genuine. It occurred to her as she replied that if she needed anything she would dial Andi or Fallon first. "I will," she replied.

"Love you."

"I love you too," Riley replied. She did love her sister. She didn't feel the need to spend boat loads of time with Mary. Riley closed her eyes. *I'm glad that's over.*

⚜ ⚜ ⚜

Fallon opened her front door. "Hey."

"Fawon!"

"Hey, buddy!"

"Sorry to just drop in on you. I was on my way to Burlington. Owen wanted to see you." *Okay, maybe I did too.*

Fallon picked up Owen. "You can drop in any time. You know that. What are you headed to Burlington for?"

"I need to go to the mall."

"The mall? Returning some of the noisy toys?" *Like maybe the chattering dinosaur.*

Riley laughed. "No. I need some new luggage."

"Luggage?"

"Yeah, for my trip home. Mine is… Well, it's not pretty."

Fallon nodded. "Feel like some company?"

"Aren't you working?"

"Nope. Not today."

"Really?"

"I promised Mom I wouldn't live at the pub. I'm betting that she has Andi keeping a calendar or something."

Riley could believe that. "No plans?"

"Not until later."

"In that case, if you think you can tolerate chicken nuggets for lunch, we'd love it. Wouldn't we, Owen?"

"Nuggets! Fawon, you get nuggets?"

"Ah, I see. McDonald's is the bonus, huh? Are you sick of my macaroni and cheese?" Fallon teased.

"Nuggets!" Owen exclaimed.

"Guess that answers that question. I don't blame you. Let me grab my jacket."

Owen followed on Fallon's heels. "Oh, you want to help?" Owen grinned.

"I can use all the help I can get."

Riley heard Fallon tell Owen that she loved nuggets too. She shook her head. *Two of a kind.*

Fallon knocked on Andi's door. She smiled when Andi opened it. *Dear God, she is gorgeous.* She hadn't been able to spend any alone time with Andi in a few days. Jake had been home for a couple of days before taking off again. Dave was due home the following week, and Jacob shortly after that. She hated imagining a summer with sporadic visits with Andi. It wasn't only the sex she would miss. Jake was typically on the road at least three weeks out of every month. Fallon had grown used to dropping in to see Andi. There were many times when they sat in front of a fire or ended up cooking dinner and talking with little more than a kiss passing between them.

"Hi," Fallon said.

"Well, get in here."

Fallon stepped through the door. She looked at Andi and tried to determine what she saw flickering in her lover's eyes.

Andi smiled and pressed her lips to Fallon's. "I'm glad you're here." *I missed you, Fallon.*

"Me too."

"Hungry?" Andi asked.

"Did you cook?"

"I promised you dinner, didn't I?"

"You did."

Andi took Fallon's hand and led her to the dining room. Fallon looked at the table. "What are we having?"

"Something I know you'll like?"

"You're making my scallops?"

Andi smiled. Jacob and Fallon had the same favorite meal —brown butter scallops with risotto. She often thought she could serve the pair the dish every night without either ever tiring of it. Each time she prepared it, Fallon would rave. Somewhere over the years, Fallon had deemed the meal hers. *I probably should rename it Fallon's Scallops.* One thing Andi was confident she had a talent for was cooking. She'd never taken a lesson. Trial and error, and endless experimentation had been Andi's teachers. Tonight, she wanted to do something special for Fallon, something memorable. She intended every moment of their evening to be memorable.

"Pour the wine and I'll finish dinner," Andi said.

Fallon poured them each a glass of wine and carried them into the kitchen where Andi was starting dinner.

"Thank you," Andi said.

Fallon leaned against the counter and watched Andi toss the scallops in the pan. "You should've been a chef or something."

"Or something?"

"Well, it's not your *only* talent," Fallon teased.

"Good to know. I'm not sure how marketable my other *skills* are."

"Oh, I think you'd be surprised how many people would be interested in them."

Andi chuckled. "I'll keep that in mind."

Fallon smiled at her lover. She loved to watch Andi in the kitchen. She loved to watch Andi with her boys. She loved to watch Andi when she was laughing or sipping her margarita.

She loved to watch Andi as Andi's body submitted to her touch. She loved to…

"What are you thinking about?" Andi asked.

"Dessert."

❧   ❧   ❧

Fallon stood behind Andi, her hands found Andi's waist. "You're so beautiful."

Andi leaned into Fallon's embrace. Could anything feel better? Could anyone make her feel the way Fallon could? The sound of Fallon's voice was like velvet. The warmth of Fallon's breath as it tickled her neck made her sigh. *Fallon.* She needed Fallon now. More than lust, beyond desire, Andi *needed* Fallon. She turned in Fallon's arms and looked in Fallon's eyes. Fallon always told her she was beautiful. *Do you see yourself?*

"What?" Fallon wondered. Her fingertips brushed an errant strand of hair from Andi's eyes.

Andi's lips pressed gently to Fallon's in reply. Tentative and hopeful, Andi's lips coaxed Fallon's to part.

Fallon fell away. The caress of Andi's tongue, the warmth and sweetness of her mouth, it made Fallon's body ache with desire. She pulled Andi closer, needing the contact unlike she ever had. What was happening to her? Her heart thudded violently, desperation gripping her soul. It was as if she were spiraling into darkness and Andi was the only light to hold onto.

Andi sensed the shift in Fallon. She pulled back slightly and pulled Fallon's sweater off, then her own. Piece by piece, between fleeting kisses and murmured promises, Andi divested them both of everything that separated them. She stepped back and let her eyes sweep over Fallon's form. Strong, even commanding, dips and curves, sensuality defined—that was Fallon. The vulnerability in Fallon's darkened eyes moved Andi unlike any touch or kiss could. She pressed Fallon back onto the bed, spreading herself across Fallon in a warm blanket of flesh. She would speak no words tonight. Tonight, she would give Fallon every piece of herself, the parts she'd kept hidden, and the places Fallon had become well-acquainted with. She'd let nothing between them, not space, not thought, not time nor questions. Her lips wandered over Fallon's throat, her eyes taking in the steady rise and fall of Fallon's chest. The swell of Fallon's breasts greeted her lips and she delighted in the arch of Fallon's back that urged her to continue.

Fallon's pulse raced. Andi's mouth encircled her nipple, swirling and teasing, tasting and sucking with loving abandon. Every nerve in Fallon's body answered Andi's request, listening and begging at the same time. Had she ever felt this way? Had Andi ever touched her this way? Fallon couldn't recall. Fallon couldn't seem to think at all. Thought had evaporated into feeling. If she was going to drown, this would be the perfect place to have it all end. Her hands took hold of Andi's head tenderly. Without the ability to form a thought, Fallon could scarcely hope to speak any words.

Andi moaned against Fallon's flesh. Fallon's body moved against hers sensually. Heat erupted over her skin and traveled deeper, down to her core. She needed Fallon tonight. She needed Fallon to know, to feel her truth; to understand that Andi had given part of herself away the first time they had kissed. That piece would forever belong to Fallon Foster. She glanced at Fallon's parted lips and let her body slide lower.

Fallon's head began to spin. Andi's fingers entered her tenderly, so softly that Fallon thought her heart might break at the sensation. What was happening to her? Andi had touched her thousands of times. She'd never felt this—not this. The gentleness of Andi's touch as she moved in and out of Fallon took Fallon's breath away. She closed her eyes. Warmth, so soft, slowly traveled the length of Fallon's need. Shouldn't she be begging? Andi's touch seemed to be pleading with her, telling her something. Fallon's hands grasped Andi's shoulders. *So, perfect. Andi.*

Tears gathered in Andi's eyes. *Fallon*. Sweet, sensitive, loving Fallon. She felt Fallon's vulnerability as it rose against Fallon's will. Andi coaxed it forward, her fragility meeting Fallon's in a dance like no other.

Fallon turned them just as her arousal began to crest. She needed to feel Andi. Andi fell into her arms gratefully. Fallon's mouth claimed her lover's, searching and speaking silently. Her fingers fell to Andi's softness, eliciting a sigh from them both. How many times had they come together? Fallon couldn't be sure. Everything seemed to vanish in an instant. Fallon's body hummed with energy, her heart churning with emotion. She felt quivers burst forward in them both. She gentled her touch slightly, following Andi's lead, needing to prolong their connection. It was strange, the ache that preceded release. It was painful, yet welcome. Andi's fingers twirled inside her and Fallon's body gave over, Andi's following close behind.

"Andi," Fallon nearly cried.

Andi breathed Fallon in, her scent, the emotions rolling off her, her presence. Fallon fell into her arms and Andi held her close. Light shaking was accompanied by a warm wetness on her breast. Andi stroked Fallon's hair. "Fallon." Andi attempted to coax Fallon. "Fallon."

Reluctantly, Fallon shifted to face her lover.

Andi's heart dropped in her chest. She pulled Fallon close and held her. She'd watched Fallon's eyes moisten on a few occasions; she'd never seen Fallon cry. She didn't need a crystal ball to know the cause—Riley Main.

"Oh, sweetheart, it was bound to happen."

Fallon's tears continued to fall. Andi's arms held her protectively, swaying her gently like a mother rocking her baby. It made Fallon's heart ache. Life had been rolling along pleasantly. Everything suddenly felt upside down—out of place. She felt as if she were drifting aimlessly. It wasn't the first-time Fallon had felt untethered. And, that is how she felt, as though she were drifting in no certain direction, lost and unable to find solid ground.

"Fallon," Andi whispered. She kissed Fallon's temple gently. "It's okay."

"No, it's not."

"Why not?"

Fallon tensed in Andi's embrace.

"Sweetheart, talk to me."

"How can I talk to you about this?"

Andi stroked Fallon's hair. She breathed in Fallon's faintly floral scent, something she was confident few people would imagine. Fallon's standard blue jeans and button down shirts always gave away a hint of her womanly assets. Her attire was generally understated. She worked hard. She was likely to be hitching a plow to a truck, building a new shed or repairing the plumbing at *Murphy's Law*, not endeavors most people equated with femininity. Fallon was all woman. She had no time for stereotypes and no care for other people's expectations about who she should be or how she should appear. Andi found those qualities sexy as hell. *I do love you, Fallon. God knows, I do.*

"You can talk to me about anything," Andi promised.

"I don't want to lose you."

Andi sighed. Change had a strange way of revealing truth. "You mean this?"

"I mean—you."

Andi looked in Fallon's eyes. There it was, the truth. What did it mean to be *in love?* Love coursed between them in power-ful waves. Not for the first time, Andi was reminded that Fallon was her closest friend, her confidante. Sex hadn't dimin-ished their friendship, it had strengthened it.

"This," Andi began softly. "Us—touching you, being with you like this... Fallon, I will miss this when it ends. I could lie to you. I won't. I don't want to lose you either."

"I know."

"I love you. It's not what you need, not forever. I know that. I've always known that. I do love you. As hard as it will be when I can't hold you again, when I can't feel you next to me, it won't change the fact that I want you in my life. Nothing could ever change that."

Fallon closed her eyes and held onto Andi. She wasn't ready to walk away from what she and Andi shared, and she was nowhere close to pursuing anything beyond friendship with Riley. So, why did she feel so afraid?

Andi closed her eyes, content to feel Fallon in her arms. Their time as lovers was approaching its end. While she could tell Fallon wasn't ready to acknowledge that; Andi felt the truth in her bones. How many more times could she hold Fallon like this; feel Fallon's flesh pressed against her? Once? Twice? A dozen more? *If only I could hold on. Oh, Fallon, I'll miss you.*

"You'll never lose me, Fallon. Just like there are parts of me I could never give you, there are parts of me no one else will ever have."

"I know." Fallon did know.

Andi inhaled a deep breath. "Stay."

Fallon lifted herself to look in Andi's eyes. She brushed her lips across Andi's softly. If only she could. The temptation to cross that line took her breath away. It was a line that kept things clear between them. If Fallon spent a night holding Andi, sleeping beside her, it would change things between them. It would entice them to see their relationship as something more than it was meant to be. Fallon had told Riley that she didn't believe you could choose to fall in love. What she failed to tell her was that she did believe you could walk away from it. She and Andi had dangled on that edge for nearly a year. A million ifs and a million more realities kept them from giving into the fall. Fallon often mused that in some other distant life Andi had been more than her lover. If Fallon ever gave her heart again it would be to someone who could give her the things she still desired. She avoided thinking about those things as much as she could. She'd buried the longing she held for a family, for someone to wake up with every morning, to fight with, to raise children with for years. Why contemplate fairy tales? Lately, those desires seemed determined to surface. Fallon fought to suppress them, to drown them in work or with sex. For a while it would quell her yearning as it had for years. Then, without her permission everything bubbled up, threatening to drown her with its force. And, every time that happened there was one name on her lips, one face in her thoughts—Riley. *Impossible*. Why was she determined to fall in love with people who would never be able to give her what she craved? Was she broken? Was Olivia right? Was she simply too idealistic? Fallon had always considered herself more of a realist than a romantic. Wasn't there a place for romance? Didn't every person privately yearn for someone to share their life with? So many questions without any answers. Fallon searched Andi's eyes, imploring her for some direction.

Andi smiled and caressed Fallon's cheek. She sighed when Fallon leaned into her touch. "I know you can't stay." The words that fell from her lips held more truth than for one moment.

"Andi…"

"I know. Stop running from it, Fallon. Stop trying to deny what you feel. And, stop worrying about me."

"I'll never stop worrying about you." *Never, Andi.*

Tears gathered in Andi's eyes. "And, I'll never stop caring for you."

"We're quite the pair, aren't we?"

"I guess we are," Andi said.

"Do you ever wonder—if we could have been…"

Andi's heart ached. *All the time.* "Wondering doesn't change anything."

"No."

"I wouldn't trade one moment we've had—not one," Andi said.

"I'm not ready to say goodbye."

"I know. That's why I have to."

Fallon's tears spilled over again.

Andi pulled her close. "Shhh."

"I don't want to be lonely again."

"I know, sweetheart. That's why we have to let this go."

"I can't…"

"You can't hide anymore, Fallon—not even here." Andi kissed Fallon's temple. "You have to give yourself a chance."

"What if…"

"There are no what if's. There's only what happens and what we do about it."

Fallon quivered in Andi's arms. "I love you, Andi." *I do. God, help me. I do.*

Andi's tears fell freely. Change was never easy. It seemed unfair. Andi had come to understand that for anything new to grow, something else had to die. That was the nature of living. "I love you too, Fallon. I love you too." *More than I can ever tell you.*

CHAPTER TWELVE

Riley opened her front door. It was nearly midnight. Her heart stopped. "Fallon?"

"It's over, Riley."

Riley was confused.

"Me and Andi. It's over."

Riley was stunned. Fallon's eyes were swollen. She led Fallon inside and enveloped her in a hug. Fallon's tears started fresh.

"Come on," Riley cooed. "Come sit down with me. Tell me what happened."

Fallon let Riley lead her to the sofa. Why was she here? Of all places, why had she come to Riley's? Regret and confusion overwhelmed her.

"Hey," Riley called softly. "What happened?"

"Nothing," Fallon replied. *And everything. I love you. That's what happened. She knows it. I love her too. How can that happen?*

Riley sighed. Andi made many denials to Riley about how she felt for Fallon. Andi loved Fallon. Riley guessed that Andi was in love with Fallon. Some part of Fallon was in love with Andi. An ending had always been inevitable. That didn't make it easy. "I'm sorry, Fallon. I know how much you care for her."

Fallon nodded. "She's right. I know she's right. Why does it hurt so much?"

"Because you love her."

Fallon's eyes filled with tears again. What was wrong with her? Were these tears endless? Is this what her mother was afraid of? And, Riley? God, she loved Riley. That hurt most of all. It was all her fault—again. Andi had quelled her loneliness, given her a place to fall and feel—feel something beyond momentary arousal and gratification. Why did she insist on falling in love with people who would never be able to give her what she desired? Riley? Just perfect, she'd broken Andi's heart, splintered her own by stupidly falling for a woman who could never love her—a straight woman. *Well, that takes the cake, Fallon.*

"Fallon," Riley whispered. "It'll be okay. I know it doesn't feel like it right now, but things will work out."

"I'm not sure what that even means," Fallon confessed.

"Andi loves you," Riley offered.

"I know."

Riley kissed Fallon's forehead. "What do you say I make us some cocoa?"

"Cocoa?"

"I'll throw some Bailey's in it for good measure."

Fallon smiled weakly. *How do you do that; make it better?*

"It's my remedy for the blues," Riley explained.

"I'm sorry, Riley."

"For what?"

"For dropping in at midnight and crying on your shoulder. I just… I didn't want to be alone."

"You don't have to be." Riley started for the kitchen and stopped. "There's a pair of your sweats in my room," she said. "From when I stayed over. Why don't you go change?"

Fallon stared at Riley.

"Well? I have extra blankets too. Go on. I seem to recall you telling me that turnabout was fair play once. I guess it's my couch's turn to host you."

Fallon chuckled. There was no point in arguing. Riley wouldn't force her, but the offer was sincere. Fallon wanted to accept. She didn't want to be alone. Somehow, she knew Riley would understand. She nodded and headed off to find the sweats.

Riley made her way to the kitchen, filled a tea kettle with water, and lit the burner. She took a deep breath and let it out slowly. A quick glance to make certain that Fallon was out of earshot and she picked up her phone.

Andi looked at the caller and sighed. "Hi, Riley."

"Are you okay?"

"She's there; isn't she?"

"She is."

"Good."

"Andi… Are you okay there…"

"I'm all right, Riley; I promise."

"Is it okay if I tell you that I think you're full of shit?"

Andi laughed. "I'd expect nothing less."

"What can I do?" Riley asked.

A tear washed over Andi's cheek. "Take care of her, Riley."

Andi's simple reply made Riley's chest ache. "I will; I promise."

I know you will, Riley. You just need to figure out what that means. "Don't worry about me."

"Too late."

Andi chuckled. "I'll see you soon, Riley."

Riley couldn't speak. She placed the phone on the counter with a sigh.

"How was Andi?" Fallon asked as she stepped into the kitchen.

Riley looked up regretfully.

"It's all right." Fallon smiled earnestly. "I don't know if you realize it, but Andi thinks of you like a daughter."

Fallon's observation should have delighted Riley. Tonight, it aroused a sense of guilt, although Riley wasn't sure why. "I didn't know."

"Mm. Like you feel about her."

"I guess I do," Riley admitted. "Or a sister."

Fallon grabbed the kettle off the burner when it whistled. "So? How is she?"

"Hurting," Riley answered honestly. "Just like you."

"We'll be okay, Riley." Fallon wasn't sure if she spoke the words for Riley's benefit or hers.

"You will be," Riley agreed. "Let me get the cocoa."

"And the Bailey's."

"And the Bailey's. Fallon?"

"Hum?"

"It really will be—all right, I mean. I know it doesn't feel that way. It will be."

Fallon nodded. *I hope so, Riley. I hope so.*

May 24ᵗʰ

"What are you up to?" Carol asked Fallon. Fallon's playful grin made her giggle. "Off to torture Riley?"

"Torture? I'm not bringing any silly string." Fallon was sure that Riley remained grateful Owen's party had taken place at Fallon's house. Fallon had been finding trails of silly string ever since the birthday party. *Still better than dealing with that talking dinosaur.*

"What?"

"Never mind," Fallon said. "You missed that part."

"Oookaaay."

Fallon shrugged.

"What are you up to, Fallon?"

"I'm not *up to* anything. I'm just picking up dinner for a friend and surprising her."

Carol stopped drying the glass in her hand, set it down and put her hands on her hips. "I don't believe it."

"What?"

"You're wooing Riley."

"Wooing? What is that; some kind of weird bird call?"

"Ha-ha. Tell me I'm wrong. You're trying to get in Riley's pants."

Fallon sobered. "No."

Carol knew which buttons to push to get the information she desired. She ought to. She spent more hours with Fallon over the last eight years than anyone. *I knew it.*

"What? Why are you looking at me like that?"

"She's terrific, Fallon."

"Who?"

"Who? Riley, you idiot."

"Yeah, she is."

"Well, I hope it all works out."

"What's that?"

"Riley."

"I'm not… Carol, we're not…"

Carol smiled. *Not yet.*

Riley had been struggling to concentrate all day. She had tried unsuccessfully to avoid thinking about the milestones of this day. The only thing staying home seemed to accomplish was making her think about it more. She'd gone as far as to pull out her wedding album. It surprised her that she felt little sadness in flipping through the pages. The images made her laugh and smile. She did miss Robert. She missed his laugh, and the way he would wink at her from across a room. She missed his off-key singing in the car and the shower. She missed his arms around her and his lips on hers. Most of all, she missed his friendship. She massaged her temples. Owen was at a friend's house. She was bored. Boredom led to thinking and that was the last thing that Riley wanted to do. She was relieved when her phone rang. An adult conversation—hell, any conversation would be welcome right now.

Jerry. Well, he is an adult. Riley answered the call. "Hi, Jerry."

"Hi. Busy?"

"Nope."

"Good. Well, not good, but, well, you know."

"What's up?" Riley asked.

"I was just wondering if you were busy, you know, later, not now, because you already said you're not busy now."

Talking to Jerry sometimes made Riley dizzy. He was very sweet. *Sweet. He is sweet.* "Other than fixing Owen dinner and probably being forced to listen to talking dinosaurs or traveling through Storybook Village, I'm open."

"Oh… That sounds… Well, I hate to intrude on your time with Owen and dinosaurs."

"Jerry? What are you asking me?"

"Oh, I was wondering if you might like to have dinner at Josiah's. I have some friends staying in Essex. Jan, she and I have known each other since birth. She and her husband, Steve wanted to catch up."

"I don't want to intrude."

"You wouldn't be. It's always a little awkward."

"Third wheel?" Riley guessed.

"Who happened to date the second wheel all through high school."

"Ah… Sure. I'll have to see if Marge is around. I'd call Andi, but… Well, Jake is home and…"

"I get it. Just let me know. I'll pick you up around six if it works for you."

"Pretty sure it will be fine. Plan on six. If something changes, I'll let you know."

"Oh, great. Thanks, Riley."

"I'll see you." Riley set down the phone. *Very sweet. Well, you get to be the fourth wheel for a change. Stepping up in the world, Riley.* She chuckled.

❧ ❧ ❧

Andi slid the papers across the kitchen table to her husband. Jake Maguire looked at them and shook his head. "Why?"

"It's time, Jake."

"Time? Is this about Fallon?"

"This is about us. It's about me."

"And Fallon," he guessed.

"I'm not seeing Fallon anymore, not the way you mean."

Jake nodded. "She broke it off?"

"Sign the papers, Jake."

"Why? Why now?"

Andi sighed.

"Because I want to move to Arizona? Why wouldn't you want to go? What's left here, Andi? The kids are gone most of the year. Don't you think we deserve to make a change now?"

We? A change? "What kind of change do you mean, Jake?"

"What?"

"It's a simple question. What kind of change? Are you planning on retiring early?"

"No…"

"Are you planning on staying home—with me?"

"Andi, you know that my job entails travel."

Andi nodded. "So, you'll be keeping the same lifestyle only we'd have our house in Arizona."

"You make it sound like a punishment."

"Is it? Is it a punishment for me?"

"What are you talking about?"

"This is my home, Jake. You aren't interested in a home."

"That's not fair," he said.

"Isn't it? It's the truth. You want to roam the world and explore all it has to offer," she said.

"I'm not the only one who's had affairs."

"No."

Jake rubbed his face. He was frustrated and confused. "Twenty-six years of marriage, Andi. Why now?"

Andi wasn't sure how to answer that. Being with Fallon had reminded her that she could feel deeply for someone other than Jake Maguire. Ironically, watching Fallon and Riley fall in love had awakened her as well. Andi didn't want to become a bitter old woman. She loved Jake. He'd been part of her life for most of it. He'd given her two children who continued to be the center of Andi's world. She was no longer the center of any of theirs. She needed to figure out who Andi was—not Andi Maguire—Andi Sherman, the young woman she'd left behind so many years ago. What part of her still existed? What did Andi Sherman want from life? If she ever hoped to discover that, Andi needed to be alone. This was her home. Whiskey Springs was the place Andi needed and wanted to be. Perhaps Fallon was not her lover, she still loved Fallon. She loved Riley and Owen. She adored Ida and Carol. She even loved Pete and Dale. This was home—her home. That was the one thing Andi did know.

"This is what I need, Jake. You don't need me."

"How can you say that?"

"For what?" Andi asked. "You're gone more than you are here. You don't have one mistress waiting for you; you're like a sailor." She chuckled. "A girl in every port."

"Don't exaggerate."

Andi sighed. "I still love you."

"Tell me what you want, Andi and I'll do it."

"This is what I want. You are who you are, Jake. That's who you've always been. I don't want to change you. I can't follow the path you want to keep walking. I can't."

Jake studied his wife's expression. Andi had always been as intelligent and confident as she was stunning. He sighed heavily. He did love her. He'd always love her. He'd taken for granted that she would always be there. "You're sure?"

Andi nodded.

Jake took a deep breath and signed the papers. He pushed them back to Andi. "I wish you'd reconsider this."

Andi squeezed his hand. "I wish I could."

❧   ❧   ❧

Fallon drove across town to Tony's Pizza to pick up dinner. Riley loved Tony's pasta and meatballs. Fallon couldn't blame her. There weren't many choices for dining in Whiskey Springs. Tony's hole in the wall pizza joint could easily deceive an unknowing visitor. People from across the area made the drive to Tony's for pizza, grinders, salads, and pasta. That's all Tony had made for the last twenty years. The worn façade of his building added charm in Fallon's opinion. The food was amazing and inexpensive. *Double win.*

She had devised the perfect plan. Riley had absently commented that she had no plans for the next few days. Fallon would arrive around six with dinner—cheese pizza for Owen. Okay, that might torture Riley slightly. But Owen was so cute when his face was covered with sauce, it was worth it. She'd offer to clean Owen up while Riley picked up from their dinner. They would read with Owen for a little while, and when he finally went to sleep, Fallon would suggest they have a glass of wine. Then she would give Riley her gifts and say, "happy birthday." Riley deserved to be celebrated.

Fallon had spent hours online searching for the perfect gift; something that sparkled and something that Riley would treasure. Riley often left her computer open when she had stayed with Fallon. Fallon had noticed one image that flashed across it repeatedly. She'd considered a million possibilities for the perfect gift. Riley was an avid reader. She read anything and everything she could get her hands on. Fallon would have thought that her friend would be tired of reading after editing books all day long. Riley explained that it was different. She loved to immerse herself in a book and escape into some foreign land with colorful characters. Fallon had seen her read everything from *Harry Potter* to Toni Morrison. Books lined the built-in shelves of Riley's living room. Every novel by Austen and King, Rowling and Tolstoy adorned the shelves. One day, Fallon hoped the shelf would hold a volume by Riley Main. And, that is how she decided on the perfect gift.

She turned the corner and started down the winding road that led to Riley's house. A stupid grin curled her lips. Was she trying to "woo" Riley? She wanted to make Riley happy, to see Riley smile. And, yes, it was true she hoped somewhere beneath it all that one day she might just be rewarded with a sweet kiss—with Riley. Fallon took a deep breath as Riley's house came into view. Who was that on the porch? Jerry? Oh, no. Riley? Riley was saying goodbye to Marge. Fallon stopped the car. *She has a date. Jesus, Fallon, how stupid are you? It's her birthday. Of course, she has a date.* Fallon felt sick. She put the car in reverse and pulled away. *What now?*

"I thought you said Fallon was spending the night with Riley?" Charlie asked Carol.

Carol nearly groaned. Her eyes found Fallon across the room with a group of young women who had been in the bar several times in the last week. She wasn't sure what was going on with Fallon. She'd gone out back and found Fallon tossing a bag and a pizza box in the dumpster. Fallon's expression told her to leave it be. Next thing she knew, Fallon was behind the bar pouring herself a beer. Moments later, the three women had walked in. Fallon had been in the corner with them ever since. *That has no good place to go.*

"I'm not sure what happened," Carol told her fiancé. One of the women had been eyeing Fallon for days. Carol had noticed it. Fallon had seemed oblivious to the attention. That was rare. Even if Fallon chose not to act on a woman's advances, she always noticed them. Carol sighed. Fallon's moods had been fluctuating like tides for days. One minute she would seem upbeat and positive, the next she was sullen, and before you could blink, Fallon would snap over some trivial bit of information. It was wholly unlike Fallon. Part of it, Carol was certain, stemmed from the relationship she had with Andi ending. Andi hadn't been in the pub since. Carol hadn't needed to ask why. She'd gotten a call from Andi. Andi knew Fallon better than anyone except Ida, even Carol, and Carol had a close friendship with her boss. Andi's voice held both concern and sorrow.

Fallon's feelings for Riley had been apparent to Carol for months. At Owen's birthday party, she'd found herself wondering when they might be headed to the altar. Fallon had been almost giddy about her plans for the evening. Something had happened. As much as Carol dreaded Fallon's wrath, she thought it was time to find out. It wasn't the cute, flirtatious blonde hanging on Fallon's every move that Carol sought to save Fallon from; it was herself.

"Do me a favor?" Carol asked Charlie.

"Sure."

"Watch the bar for a minute?"

"Where are you going?"

Probably to my death or the unemployment line. "I'm going in."

"You're kidding," Fallon laughed. "You're renting the Bath's cabins at the pond?"

"Yeah, why?"

Fallon shook her head. "Oh, nothing." She wondered what Dora and Dick Bath might think if they knew lesbians were enjoying the fruits of their labor. She sniggered. If the night went the way she expected, Fallon would be enjoying some fruit in the Bath's cabin. That brought her a degree of sick satisfaction.

"Hey," Carol tugged on Fallon's arm.

"Oh, hey. Carol. This is Deb, Trish, and Aubrey."

"Hi," Carol greeted the trio evenly.

"They're renting those two cabins the Bath's own down at Morton Pond."

"Oh? Nice," Carol said a bit dismissively. She wanted to roll her eyes at the way Aubrey's hand not so subtly fingered Fallon's arm. *Ugh. You aren't in the same league as Andi or Riley.* "Can I borrow you for just a minute?" Carol requested.

"Sure," Fallon said. "I'll be right back," she told Aubrey.

Aubrey stretched to place her lips in front of Fallon's. "I certainly hope so."

Carol thought she might wretch. *I can't believe that works.* She walked a few feet to the side door of the pub and stepped outside.

Fallon followed her friend. "What's up?" Fallon asked.

"I don't know; you tell me."

"Tell you what?"

"What's going on with you?" Carol asked.

"I was enjoying a beer."

Carol stared at Fallon. "Why aren't you at Riley's?"

Fallon's face contorted. "She's busy."

"She's busy?"

"Yeah. You know—busy."

"Uh-huh. What did she say when you showed up?"

Fallon was growing anxious. Talking about her trip to Riley's unsettled her for reasons she had no desire to explore with Carol or anyone else. There were things she was eager to explore—things called Aubrey. "She didn't say anything."

"What?"

"I didn't talk to her."

"Lost me."

"I pulled up; she was walking out with Jerry."

"Jerry? Jerry Walker?"

Fallon made no comment.

"So, you just left?"

"I dropped some things off on the porch after they were gone."

"So, she went out; so what?"

"Exactly. It's her life."

Carol sighed. "You know, Fallon, you really can be thick."

"What the fuck does that mean?"

"If you're so crazy about Riley, maybe you should tell her."

"I'm sure Jerry has that covered. Is there anything else?"

Carol took a step toward the door. "You know; if she means that little to you that you'll just walk away because she happens to spend time with someone else, maybe she'd be better off with Jerry." She shook her head. "Go play with Aubrey."

"I will."

Carol shook her head again. *Sometimes, Fallon—sometimes.*

❧   ❧   ❧

"I'm glad you were free," Jerry said.

"I'm glad you called."

"Really?"

Riley grinned. "Yes, really. I needed to get out."

"I can't believe that Charlie and Carol set a date for the wedding already."

"I can."

"Really?"

Jerry certainly like the word really. *Not like Fallon's kerfuffle.* Fallon seemed to have fallen in love with the word kerfuffle. She would use it whenever the opportunity presented itself. Riley had asked why she had so much affection for the word.

"I don't know," Fallon told her. "I just like the way it sounds—like I'm smart."

Riley chuckled. As if Fallon wasn't intelligent. She suspected Fallon found the word fun to say. "You know, there are a plethora of under-utilized words, Fallon."

"Ohh, could there be a plethora of kerfuffles, though?"

"I don't think so."

Fallon huffed. "That would be fun to say."

"Riley?"

"What?"

"The wedding?"

"Oh, yeah." *That could turn into a kerfuffle.* She chuckled.

"Did that wine go to your head?" Jerry asked as he pulled into Riley's driveway.

"No. I'm sorry, Jerry. I was just thinking about something."

"It's okay. Listen, I had a nice time."

Riley smiled. Everything about Jerry was nice. Electric? No. Nice? Very. "Me too," she said.

He leaned over and placed a light kiss on Riley's lips.

Riley offered him another smile. *Nice. Just—nice.* "Thanks for dinner."

"I'll call you."

"Sounds good," Riley said as she stepped out of the car. *Oh, Riley... He is a very nice man. What is wrong with that?* She chuckled. *I think I'd prefer a kerfuffle.*

❦   ❦   ❦

Fallon followed Aubrey into the cabin. Before she could speak, Aubrey's mouth claimed hers with a desperate kiss. Fallon welcomed it. Fallon welcomed anything that might have the power to banish images of Riley Main. Who needed love? Where did that lead? It led directly to loneliness, that's where it led. How many lessons did a person need? She shed her jacket and tossed it carelessly aside. Aubrey's hands were everywhere all at once. Fallon immersed herself in the sensation that was pure, unapologetic lust. She wasn't seeking tenderness. She intended to touch every inch of the woman kissing her. She'd tear away the cloth barriers between them if need be.

"Mmm." Aubrey moaned into Fallon's mouth. She'd been watching Fallon for days. She'd come back to her cabin and she would imagine Fallon's lips covering her body, imagine her hands covering Fallon's breasts. Her fingers would play in time with the images. She wanted Fallon Foster. She wanted Fallon Foster to throw her up against the wall and take what she wanted. She would not be disappointed.

Fallon practically ripped the blouse from Aubrey's body. It got thrown into a growing heap of clothing. Aubrey reached for Fallon. Fallon grabbed her hands and pressed her against the wall, holding Aubrey's hands over her head. Her mouth crashed into Aubrey's demanding entry. Her teeth toyed with Aubrey's lower lip before descending to her neck and finally to a soft pink nipple.

"Fuck!" Aubrey called out.

Fallon sucked and nipped at the pink flesh until Aubrey strained against her. She pressed her full weight against the younger woman. "I'm going to make you come like you never have."

Warmth flooded Aubrey's veins and pooled between her legs. *Yes.* That's what she wanted.

Fallon unbuttoned Aubrey's jeans and lowered them. She wasted no time. Her fingers found the wet, eager softness she expected. She played for a moment, teasing the woman against her, circling and toying.

"Fuck, Fallon…"

"Fuck?" Fallon asked. "Is that what you want? You want me to fuck you right now?"

"Yes. Fuck yes."

Fallon's fingers thrust into her lover forcefully.

"Yes," Aubrey hissed as Fallon's fingers built a steady rhythm. Her fantasies about Fallon paled by comparison to the woman now moving inside her.

Fallon lost herself. It felt good—all of it. She absorbed the sound of Aubrey's sighs and pleas. She inhaled the scent of arousal and unbridled lust that permeated the room. Everything she felt, everything she questioned she poured into this young woman. This woman wanted nothing more from Fallon than for Fallon to make her feel good, and that is all Fallon desired. She let her thumb press the small sensitive bud that she knew would send Aubrey soaring and pressed her fingers deeper. Aubrey's body trembled. Fallon steadied her with the weight of her body and continued her thrusting.

"Harder!"

A pulse of excitement traveled through Fallon. Harder it would be.

"Fuck yes!"

Fallon devoured Aubrey's cries with her mouth. Aubrey shook violently. Fallon's kiss softened.

"Jesus," Aubrey whispered. "Do I get to return the favor?"

Fallon turned them and led Aubrey to the bed. She shed her remaining clothing and climbed on top of the young woman.

Aubrey let out a primal groan. "I'm going to lick every inch of you."

Fallon grinned. "Do it."

❧   ❧   ❧

"Thanks for watching Owen."

Marge smiled brightly. "You don't ever have to thank me."

"He loves having you here," Riley said. She wasn't being kind; it was the truth. Owen adored Marge.

"Oh, I almost forgot." Marge ran over to the kitchen table. "This was on the step."

Riley puzzled over the gifts that Marge handed her. "What is this?"

"I don't know. The card is addressed to you. Maybe a present that was missed at Owen's party."

Riley shrugged. "Maybe. Thanks again." She set the boxes on the sofa.

"Did you still want me to come over next Wednesday?"

Riley smiled. "Please."

"Another date with Jerry?"

"No."

"Getting into trouble with Fallon?"

Riley laughed. "It might be Fallon you should worry about. I'm cooking her dinner."

"Another bet?"

"No, an overdue promise."

Marge nodded. "If you need anything before then…"

"You'll be the first to know." Riley bid Marge goodnight and closed the door.

Riley closed her eyes for a second and took a deep breath. A glass of wine was in order, a glass of wine and maybe a good book. She made her way to the kitchen and opened a bottle of Riesling. *Something sweet.* Riley wandered back to the sofa and collapsed onto it, ready for a few moments of complete silence and relaxation. She glanced at the packages she had placed there. *Fallon.* The handwriting on the card was unmistakable.

Riley,
I discovered by accident that it's your birthday.

Riley sighed.

I'm not sure if there's a reason that you didn't want to celebrate, but I wanted you to know that I think you should be celebrated.

Riley smiled.

I know that you probably think what I said in that crazy proposal Andi roped us into was all made up. I really am not very good with words. That was true. You're the aspiring writer. I just serve drinks.

"You do a lot more than serve drinks," Riley commented.

It's also true that I don't want to imagine my life without you in it. You've become my best friend. I look forward to our dinners and our late-night conversations.

"And, sledding down my hill, and me doing your laundry."

Plus, I get help with my laundry.

Riley laughed.

You give to everyone, Riley. You help everyone without ever asking for a thing. I wanted you to have something just for you, something to let you know how special I think you are.

"Fallon…"

You mentioned that you like sparkly things. Proposals aside, I thought I'd look for something that fit the bill. I hope you like it. I know that you love Tolstoy, so that's what gave me the idea. You really should write that book you've been talking about. I know I would read it. Maybe this will help. Happy Birthday, Riley.
Love,
Fallon

Riley picked up the packages Fallon had left. She tore the paper away from the first and held her breath. Slowly, she opened the lid of the box to reveal a stunning fountain pen, a *Mont Blanc* limited edition honoring Leo Tolstoy. *Oh, my God,*

Fallon, what did you do? She'd been looking at them online, day-dreaming. Who would spend a thousand dollars on a pen? Apparently, the answer to that question was Fallon Foster. She opened the next gift and smiled. It was a stunning leather journal. Riley's fingertips traced over the cover. *Fallon.* She picked up her phone, pressed the familiar contact and waited.

"Hey, you've reached Fallon. I'm probably pouring at the pub. You know what to do if you don't want to come find me."

"Hi," Riley began softly. "I just opened your gifts." Riley took a breath. "Fallon, they're… They're amazing." *Just like you.* "I don't know how you knew. I didn't tell anyone. It's just… Today isn't an easy day for me. I was going to call you. Jerry called and offered to take me to dinner. I just needed to get out of the house. I never expected you to… I don't know what to say. You are…Well, I feel the same way about you. I don't want to think about not having you in my life." *I don't.* "Call me when you get this. Okay?" Riley's fingers danced over the journal again. She took a deep breath. "Dinner, tomorrow? I'd like to see you. I… I miss you. Call me."

Riley placed the phone beside her and looked at the presents in her lap. *Fallon. What would I do without you?*

❧ ❧ ❧

Fallon threw her jacket onto the passenger seat and closed the door of her truck. She steadied her breathing and gripped the steering wheel. Why did she suddenly feel worse than she had when she'd walked into *Murphy's Law?* A faint buzzing drew her attention.

"Hi, Mom."

"Hi, Mom? Where are you? And who is Aubrey?"

"What?"

"You called me Fallon, two hours ago—although I'm not sure *why* you called me."

"I didn't call you. Oh, shit. I must've dialed you somehow when I…"

"I don't want to know," Ida said.

"Then why did you call back?"

"What are you doing?" Ida asked.

"Something tells me you already know the answer to that question."

"I thought you were surprising Riley for her birthday."

"Yeah, so did I."

"What happened?"

"Jerry happened."

Ida took a deep breath. "Jerry happened."

"Yeah. I went over and she was getting in Jerry's car. I guess he rates enough to spend her birthday with."

Ida wished she could crawl through the phone and smack Fallon. "Stop pouting."

"What?"

"You heard me. What makes you think Riley told him it was her birthday?"

"Didn't you hear what I said? She was getting into *his* car."

"So?"

"Mom…"

"I probably should keep my mouth shut."

"Probably."

"Right, probably. I'm not going to."

Fallon groaned.

"If you love Riley, you'd better be prepared to fight for her."

"Fight for her? Why should I have to fight for her?"

"Fallon, honestly. We all have to fight to keep our relationships secure."

Fallon sighed.

"You blame yourself for Olivia. You can say whatever you want; you do. Don't say a word right now, you listen to me. You didn't fight for her. Maybe that was because somewhere inside you knew it wasn't the right relationship for you."

Fallon closed her eyes.

"You didn't fight for Andi either."

"Mom, Andi…"

"I said, listen to me. Andi wouldn't have let you. I know that hurt you."

"Mom, please…"

"Fallon, someone needs to say this to you. It's safest if I do."

"Why? Because you're five-hundred miles away?"

"I'm not scared of you, Fallon."

Fallon chuckled.

"You don't have to say a word. It's written all over your face. You love Riley." She heard Fallon sigh.

"Riley's seeing Jerry."

"Yes, well seeing someone has a different meaning for most people than it does for you."

"What does that mean?"

"Do you really think that sleeping with every moderately attractive woman who passes through town is going to make you forget Andi or fall out of love with Riley?"

"Is that what you think I'm doing?"

"Aren't you?"

"It was one night, Mom."

"I know you, Fallon. That's not what you want. Riley's been through a lot."

"And? Riley's straight."

"Oh? Told you that, did she?"

"No, but… Jesus, Mom she was married. She has a kid."

Ida had to shake her head to clear the clouds. "Olivia's married with kids."

"Thanks for reminding me. Olivia is a lesbian."

"Andi's married and has kids." There was no reply. "How do you know what Riley feels if you don't ask her?"

"Ask her? Are you crazy? I don't need to ruin that friendship."

"Well, traipsing off with coeds might just do that for you."

"Mom."

"I think you are underestimating Riley. You might remember that I've had almost forty years to decode your logic. She's had less than six months. Give it some time, Fallon. If you're so worried about Jerry Walker, do something about it."

"I don't want to lose her too."

"None of us want to lose, Fallon. We all wish every ending could be happy. Loving someone ensures that at some point, one of you or both of you will have to say goodbye. If it's not life that causes that, it's death."

"Then what's the point?"

"Well, the thing about love is when the ending comes it's all you have left to hold onto. Endings come whether we let ourselves love or not. What you have left to hold onto is what matters."

"Memories? That seems hollow."

"Does it? It's not, Fallon. It's a lot more than memories. Loving someone changes you. It takes time to see that when you're hurting. It's a scary thing—loving someone, giving yourself over to it when you know it could lead you to pain one day. Running from it will hurt as much as following it ever could. Give yourself a chance, Fallon."

"You sound like Andi."

"Andi's a smart woman who happens to love you."

Fallon's eyes welled with tears. "I know."

"Enough to know it was time to let go. Don't make that for nothing."

Fallon took a deep breath. "I do."

"You do?"

"I love Riley."

"You don't say. It's not me who needs to know that."

"I don't think she's ready for that, Mom."

"Then give it the space it needs for now. Just don't give it too much space."

"Mom?"

"Yes?"

"Andi…"

"Fallon, you have to let Andi go now, not just for you, but because she needs you to. She's still a young woman, even if she doesn't think so. She deserves a chance to find out who she is."

Fallon was puzzled by her mother's comment. "Is she…"

"Let it go, Fallon. She'll come to you when she's ready. Give her time."

"I don't know how."

"You do. I haven't told you one thing that you didn't know. You just needed to hear someone say it."

Fallon chuckled. Maybe she did. "I guess I should say thanks."

"You can thank me by not butt dialing me to 'Oh, yes, Fallon' being screamed in my ear."

Fallon cringed. "Promise."

"Thank you. Say hello to Riley and Owen for me."

"I will. If you talk to Andi…"

"She knows, Fallon. Trust me; she knows."

"I'll talk to you soon."

"I certainly hope so."

Fallon disconnected the call. She was about to set down the phone when she noticed the voicemail. Riley's voice came over the line.

"Hi. I just opened your gifts. Fallon, they're… They're amazing. I don't know how you knew. I didn't tell anyone. It's just… Today isn't an easy day for me. I was going to call you. Jerry called and offered to take me to dinner. I just needed to get out of the house. I never expected you to… I don't know what to say. You are…Well, I feel the same way about you. I don't want to think about not having you in my life. Call me when you get this. Okay? Dinner, tomorrow? I'd like to see you. I… I miss you. Call me."

Fallon took a deep breath and looked at the time. *It's worth a try.*

"Fallon?" Riley answered her phone.
"Did I wake you up?"
"Not really, I was just lying here."
"I got your voicemail."
"I got your gifts."
"I hope you like them."
"Fallon… They're… I love them."
"I was calling to… I know, I've been kind of an ass the last few days."
"You have?" Riley teased.
"I'm sorry."
"You don't need to apologize. I know you've been hurting."
Not for all the reasons you think. "The thing is, I missed you too."
Riley smiled. "Is that so?"
"Yeah, it is."
"Me or Owen and all his new toys?"
Fallon answered honestly. "I miss both of you—and the toys."
"I can't believe it."
"So, um… Is that offer still good for dinner to… Well, later today?"
"It is."
"Great. I'll bring the wine."
"I'll make sure *Super Why* is in the DVD player."
"Who could refuse that offer?"
"Not you."
Fallon laughed. "I'll see you later."

"You will. Fallon?"

"Yeah?"

"What you wrote in that card… I… You'll never know how much that meant to me—all of it."

I love you, Riley. "I meant every word."

Riley closed her eyes. *I know you did.* "I'll see you around six?"

"I'll be there." Fallon set down her phone and closed her eyes. *I'll be there, Riley.*

The End

Coming February 2018
The story continues in

CIGAR CLUB

Made in the USA
Columbia, SC
27 August 2020